First Ladies C

Be More
Than
Blessed!

Nadia Mathews

First Ladies Club

Rocks, Rings and Resurrections

The Riveting Sequel to First Ladies Club: When the Church Hats Come Off

First Ladies Club: Rocks, Rings and Resurrections

Dedication

There are so many things that I could say about the journey to finish this book... I have been at the highest emotional place and at the bottom. My truth is that in all of it, in everyplace in my life God has been there. He has sent me His best guardian angels in the form of my amazing friends. To My King, my Boaz and my everything wrapped in muscles Lee Mathews: I love you with all that God has given me to love you. You are my soul mate and the wind in my SWAG! I am so grateful that in the midst of the dark storms of our life that we held onto each other. You were the ears to every character and every word and I love you for the sound of your enthusiasm with every chapter. I am here, because God has given you a Word for my life.

My family is such a blessing. To my parents, Jackie Blount and Murry Blount who keep me lifted up before God and take care of my girls like they birthed them. You two are the epitome of what grandparents should be. THANK YOU!! I have the most beautiful daughters, 3 girls and 2 bonus babies. Laila, Kayla, Audrey, Tanaya, Rodnae. You all keep me at my computer, and on the grind to build a legacy for your future.

To my editor and my sister, Sierra (Going to rule the world one day) Starks there are no words to say how much I appreciate you. Your hard work has been priceless. I know that I have been a thorn in your side for over 3 years, but you've remained a blessing to my life. All the texts, calls and carrier pigeons I sent out to find you were all worth it. There would be NO BOOK if it wasn't for your love of the project, dedication and amazing gifts. I am blessed that God chose me to work with you. Your future is brighter than you know. Keep shining and watch God do all He has promised you.

To my Best Friend and Pastor Lady Keisha Randolph: We've been riding together forever! You have been a supportive voice throughout this process and words can't express my gratitude. You are a beacon of light in the world. I love you, because more than a friend, you are my sister. To my extended Moore and Smith family, I love you for always supporting me in whatever I do.

To my Life Design Coach Apostle Jasonn Randolph: Thank you for listening to all my crazy stories and telling me I'm not crazy while taking mental notes at the levels of my craziness. Thank you for showing me the beauty in everything and for inviting me into your family. We are eternally grateful for your wise counsel and direction from God. What you've done in the life of the Mathews has been nothing short of miraculous! This is your season for greatness, and I am honored to share this journey as your mentee and spiritual daughter.

To the women that always support me, pray for me and hold me up when I want to say uncle. THANK YOU!!! Jew-Jew, Lona, , Shannel Wheeler (the baddest graphic designer in the land..OMG!!!) Monique, Nyasia (My PUSHER) Courtney, Tiberia, Samantha, Dr. Lateefah Goines(a.k.a Lala Da queen), Prophetess Iantha Taylor (the original fire starter) and every other blessing to my life!

There are a million Thank You's I could say, but none greater than saying thank you to God first. Then I extend it to each of you for believing in my vision and purchasing my book. May your life be blessed by the First Ladies and my prayer is that you feel every emotion I felt as I poured myself into this book.

Nadia Mathews

www.nadiamathewsspeaks.com

Nadia Mathews

Grace and Peace Productions

First Ladies Club; Rocks, Rings and Resurrections

Copyright © 2014 by Nadia Mathews

All Rights reserved.

No part of this book can be reproduced or transmitter in any form or by any means-electronic, mechanical, photocopy, recording or otherwise-without written permission from the author.

Scripture quotations are from Zondervan King James Bible

Editing: Sierra Starks & Tanikka Bradley

Cover Design: Massive Burns Studios & Shannel Wheeler

Praise for First Ladies Club: When The Church Hats Come Off

Goodreads Reviews

This book was so exciting, I am not going to share much with you because it is seriously a must read. You have to find out what is behind the hats of the first ladies coming off and what happens when it does. What do the first ladies actually do beside dress to the nine and give that superior look.....well this book gives you both sides or should I say all side. Do yourself a favor get the book and go through all the changes with the ministries....you will love it. I am truly waiting on the continuation or sequel to this story.

I truly enjoyed this book. All of the first ladies had a story. You sometimes forget that first ladies are just humans like everyone else in church. Nadia did a great job of showing this. Would recommend this book.

Amazon Reviews

These ladies' stories have been brought to life by Nadia. She enables the reader to feel their sorrow and pain as well as relish in their joy! I didn't put my kindle down until the book was done, and even then I wanted more. Can't wait for pt 2!

The truth behind the mask many women wear; the more meticulous the outside appearance is proves that a mess is brewing inside. this story reveals the true sacrifice a woman makes when she marries a man in the ministry but also teaches forgiveness and redemption.

NATASHA

"Will you marry me?"

Over the last six months, those words replayed like a singsong lyric in Natasha's head.

She had spent many days in therapy discovering who she was after losing her husband, Shawn, so suddenly. She was grateful that she had such support from the ladies of Deborah's Daughters, a "First Ladies club" that offered her much solace in times of need. Each one of her fellow sister-friends in the faith seemed happy and content in their own lives—enough to transfer some happiness to her newly widowed life.

Natasha's phone rang interrupting her thoughts. She found it on her bed and answered the call.

"Hello?" Natasha sat on the edge of her bed and put her earpiece in.

"Hey Natasha!" It was Amauri, fellow member of Deborah's Daughter. "Shenae, and Lynette are all on the line. What are you doing today?"

"Hey ladies," she greeted them warmly. "I'm going to another meeting with the attorney today."

It was a meeting she was dreading, honestly. The past half year, her husband's lawyer's office had been her second home. Signatures, contract modifications, updates—it was as if Shawn was still controlling her life from the grave.

"Henry's office again?" Shenae chimed in. "Will you be at our meeting later?"

Deborah's Daughters met often at their favorite coffee shop to fellowship with one another, lay burdens down, come together in prayer, and just enjoy each other's company. It was one of the things keeping Natasha sane in her constantly changing life.

"Of course I'll be there," Natasha answered.

"Awesome. We have so much to talk about," Lynette said. "We're finalizing some of the plans for Amauri and Bishop Paden's going away party."

"Ah, that's right," Natasha remembered.

It had recently been announced that Amauri and her husband would be moving back to their home state of New York to oversee their former congregation. The date was fast approaching and Deborah's Daughters were throwing the two a going away party soon.

"Have we confirmed everything with the event planner?" Natasha asked. "Shenae?"

"What?" Shenae answered, obviously distracted. "Um, yes, I think so."

Shenae had just received a call on the other line from her incarcerated husband, Leon. She was disgusted with him and the double life he'd been leading during their marriage—so much so that she couldn't bear to call him "Lee" any longer. It was a formal wedge he'd forced her to drive between them months ago. Now, if only he could stop calling her and sign the divorce papers her lawyer drafted.

"Oh, Amauri, I can't believe that you are leaving us," Natasha whined. "Are you sure you have to?"

"I know."

"Really!"

"Don't go."

The ladies all chimed in to express their sorrow.

"We have to do what God has called us to do," Amauri gave a response typical of her personality. "This isn't about us."

She fought back the tears and paused before continuing.

"I don't want to leave you all either," she finally let out.

It had been three weeks since Bishop Paden told Amauri that God was calling them back to New York to help the struggling ministry they'd built. Since that announcement, though, Paden had become more irritable than usual. Amauri just couldn't figure it out. She'd spent time praying for him, and she was sure that God would show her what was going on.

"Ladies, I have to go!" Natasha exclaimed, looking at her nightstand clock. "I have to get to the meeting. Please pray for me. I hate these meetings. Henry—he's so…greasy looking."

"We'll pray, for sure," Amauri said.

"Bye. See you beautiful ladies later," Lynette said.

"Bye."

"Bye."

Natasha ended the call and walked to her closet to prepare an outfit. On the way there, she passed the full-length mirror and stood in front of it, disapproving the giant circles around her eyes. Clearly, the insomnia was taking its toll. Her hair was pulled back into a lazy bun, causing strands to fall into her round face. She definitely felt as dry as she looked these days.

She stood there a moment longer, replaying the four words that kept her up at night.

"Will you marry me?"

Donte, the armor bearer of her deceased husband, had become her best friend since Shawn's passing. He'd been so sure when he popped the question to her, but his proposal had left Natasha feeling lost and uncertain. In her eyes, Donte was her best friend, a confidante, and a father figure for her daughter, Nivea. In the eyes of Natasha's congregation, however, his title was "the armor bearer of our former pastor (God rest his soul)."

Shawn pastored a mega church, a massive congregation, and those members even kept Natasha a detainee in her former position of First Lady, as if he hadn't died. All those former titles only fueled her indecision in taking a leap toward her future. What would it look like to the tens of thousands of members if she married Shawn's armor bearer?

"Ugh." It was all Natasha could muster as she looked away from her reflection.

She opened her closet doors with the weight of the past months heavy on her shoulders. Donte had become a force in her life since Shawn's tragic, sudden death. He was always there with his strength when things got tough. And he was always there with his laughter when she wanted to crawl in a hole in memory of how counterfeit her marriage really was. In the weeks following Shawn's death, Natasha wasn't sure how she would get the strength to get back up again, but she seemed to manage. Nivea was nearly 18 years old and a rising basketball star. The thought of her only child made Natasha smile. Donte had been as much of a father to her as Shawn had been. She couldn't lose him; she wouldn't allow it, but getting past the invisible rocks being thrown at her when members saw the two together was another thing. She felt their accusing stares during service when she and Donte sat next to each other.

"Who cares, Natasha?" she said to herself, deep in her thoughts again.

She wondered, though, if Donte wasn't also feeling the pressure of their judgmental eyes. He'd become so distant in the last few weeks. He was rarely over for lunch and dinner; he'd been busier than usual. Last week, she was up late waiting for him to come over for dinner. He showed up hours late, with infinite apologies, but could she blame him? He'd been waiting six months for her decision. Meanwhile, Natasha was just trying to decide how to start the conversation with God about it.

"So, God, I was wondering if I can marry my husband's armor bearer?"

"Heavenly Father, I know that I should still be mourning the death of my husband, but Donte is a great candidate to replace him."

"Jesus, take the wheel."

Natasha scoffed. She had been putting Donte off, steadily avoiding the question, and trying to make him understand that it wasn't the right time for either of them to even be thinking about a relationship. But a lot of time had passed since Donte had uttered those words in his kitchen. Since then, she had remained focused on gathering the remnants of her widowed life. Shawn and the surprises he left her were enough to keep her busy these days: his last will and testament, a surprise love child, and this overflowing bank account with enough money to sustain her and Nivea for the rest of their lives.

This morning, she'd once again be dealing with Shawn's last wishes, she was sure. Her husband's attorney called her to once again set up a meeting. She'd opt for something regal to wear because she didn't know the exact grounds of this meeting or who else would be in attendance. The weather outside had been mild, the leaves nearly turning their golden yellows and deep oranges. The season change happening outside her window meant that it was time for something new, but the familiarity of her First Lady attire would have to do today.

It was a far dig into her closet to find the remaining treasure of her former everyday attire. The days were long gone of Natasha's overbearing husband dressing her. He was always overly concerned with her clothes and appearance, scrutinizing her taste in colors and fabrics.

My First Lady would never wear that.

Remembering those words often made her cringe. She combed through the hangers, mindful of how she never felt good enough for Shawn. Natasha had forgotten her love for a great pair of fitted jeans and a sweater until the day she realized that she wasn't being watched anymore—at least, not as much. But, she had begun to realize that her faith wasn't measured by her clothes. In fact, the first things to go were those big, fancy First Lady hats Shawn forced her to wear. As soon as she'd given those to charity, she began to feel like she could finally just be in the crowd.

Natasha sighed, finally stumbling upon something suiting for the occasion. A pink twill coat and matching pencil skirt would show she meant business, she thought, pulling them from the closet and laying them on her bed. She'd wear her hair in a tight bun and adorn her delicate fingers with fancy gloves, she decided, and continued getting ready.

Along with Natasha's elegant wardrobe, one of the last remnants of her past life was her Mercedes. It was a present from her husband, his-and-hers luxury vehicles. She'd donated his to charity. She snickered to herself; people probably thought she was crazy for not claiming a small fortune from it.

She opened the door of her car, remembering her humble beginnings. She had almost nothing when Shawn met her, so she was indeed blessed to be a blessing these days.

Once behind the wheel, she sat there for a moment. The car felt different. Natasha looked around and saw it was neater than usual. She pulled down her visor and found a note from Donte.

Try to keep it clean this time! Love, D.

Of course, he'd cleaned her car.

"He's perfect," she let out a long sigh, starting the engine and beginning her commute. "Why can't I just commit to him?"

She knew the answer. It was probably because, for most of her life, people looked at her with looks of shame. She'd been a single mother in the church years ago, raising her daughter in a dumpy neighborhood. When Pastor Shawn approached her for dinner after his wife died, she'd literally jumped at the chance to be a First Lady. She was being rescued, and even though she didn't want to admit it, she needed him. Being a First Lady meant beautiful dresses and constant admiration, yes, but she'd finally have a father for Nivea. Her daughter was the most important person in the world to her, and if she'd have to take on a few stares for her decision, she would. And Shawn had been so good to her when they were courting. It was only after they'd been married that he changed so drastically. But everyone told her that's what relationships do; they change, they evolve over time. So, she just excused his behavior.

The mothers of the church told her that she should continue giving her husband a home-cooked meal and sex three times a week, and he'd come around. She felt silly, but she followed all their advice. She was left with a refrigerator of leftovers and an empty bed most nights. But he'd given her daughter all she could ask for, and that was what mattered to Natasha the most. What she hadn't thought about, however, was the magnitude of the title "First Lady." She'd been so caught up with the mirage of her life, she'd totally missed that her husband was less interested in her and more interested in having an image too. Shawn's goals and ambitious never included her. He was caught up in portraying the image of this distinguished religious leader. And Natasha just smiled her pretty smile and wore her pretty hats and endured the heartbreak.

He was a good father, she told herself as she pulled into a parking spot outside of the attorney's office. Shawn loved Nivea just as much as he loved his own twins.

Natasha pulled down the visor again to check her makeup. Donte had never asked her to be anything more than herself; she'd been thankful for that. Looking at her reflection with satisfaction for the first time that morning, she put on her best smile and began to make her way to the eight-story building on Peachtree Street.

On the outside, the building looked simple, but behind the revolving doors, it was something else entirely. The security guard wore a suit, discreetly hiding a firearm in the rear of his ensemble. Natasha only knew this because he'd once pulled it on an irate husband who started a brawl with his wife's attorney. The windows in the lobby were adorned with burgundy drapes. Modern art was scattered around the walls. The sofas were cream and cold like the feel of the lawyers, associates, and paralegals that walked the halls. Here, the attorneys had to meet their clients in the lobby. No one could walk past the armed gentleman in black without a badge or prior clearance.

"Hello, I'm here to see Attorney Henry Rossi," Natasha said, approaching the security guard's station at the front of the office.

From the many stares and reverential looks she'd received as she walked in, Natasha could tell she'd done a great job putting herself together without Shawn's assistance. Her bun was perfectly straight in the center of her head with the softness of the wisps of her hair falling into her face. She'd taken care to apply each palette of makeup, mixing the right colors according to both the weather and trend. She'd even worn diamond earrings and sensible two-inch heeled shoes. Natasha quickly reminded herself that she dressed to play the part she was hoping to leave behind soon, preferably after this meeting with Henry.

"Yes, of course," replied the security guard.

Jordan, as noted on his nametag, put down the Living section of the newspaper he was reading and took Natasha in for a second. The look he gave her was one of both recollection and amazement. She looked gorgeous today.

"Mrs. Shawn Winters, correct?" he responded with a full smile, grabbing the phone's receiver and dialing Henry's receptionist

Natasha winced and recovered immediately. Hearing his name out loud was another nail in the coffin of her future. Was that what the world would always know her as?

She nodded politely as Jordan relayed the message and hung up.

"Mr. Rossi will be down shortly," he told her, rising from his post and meeting her to offer her a seat on the couches. "Would you like a beverage while you wait?"

"No thanks. I'll stand," Natasha responded, removing her gloves. She walked to admire a painting on the wall. Jordan followed, his eyes making their way from her stocking-clad ankles up to her backside.

"Far From a Fairytale," Natasha softly read the name written under the piece of artwork. She turned to ask Jordan the name of the artist, expecting him to still be manning the door. Instead, she found him two steps behind her, clearly distracted.

"Excuse me," Natasha found pardoning herself, interrupting his sinful thoughts. She saw two people behind him walk into the office without so much as flashing a badge at the empty security stand.

Immediately, she was taken aback by Jordan's lack of concern for his job. She hated seeing people whose sole purpose it was to protect her occupied with Living sections in the newspaper or other distractions. She wanted to tell him that he was given a state mandated break to read the paper, not on her time when his job required his full attention.

"Mrs. Winters," Natasha heard Henry's loud voice as he opened the doors to the lobby.

Henry walked over to Natasha and grabbed her hand as Jordan hurriedly shuffled back to his post.

"You're a vision in pink," he said admiringly.

Natasha smiled and gave him a simple salutation. It was good to know that she still had a special something that made men see her. She was a woman of God, but she was still a woman.

"It's always a pleasure seeing you. Please follow me," Henry said extending his pudgy fingers toward the office doors.

"Henry, I hope this meeting is quick. I have so much to do today," Natasha said.

She decided she'd skip the pleasantries and the over-politeness today. She just wanted to know what the two hadn't settled yet. She'd been called in over the past months to sign an agreement regarding Shawn's twins, the love child from his affair, a settlement form regarding the church, the list went on and on.

"It shouldn't take long, Mrs. Winters," Henry said as they reached the elevator.

The two rode in silence to the floor his office was housed on. Natasha could tell that he'd just sprayed on cologne because the strong smell tingled her nose. Her gloves came in handy and she held them to her nostrils, holding back the urge to sneeze. The invasion of the aroma fought harder to invade her senses.

"The elevator," Henry began, "it always has a smell."

Natasha fought the urge to roll her eyes and retort, "The smell is you, sir," but she refrained. It wasn't appropriate. And if she learned anything from her former life, it was the ability to know when something was grossly inappropriate and appropriate. She kept her composure until the elevator doors opened and allowed her a breath of fresh air.

As they walked down the hall toward his office, Natasha gave Henry the once-over. His custom fitted navy blue suit stood out to her as only the kind financed by high-end clients like her deceased husband. She'd seen his overpriced shoes in a popular men's magazine that came to her home monthly. It was Shawn's subscription but was still being forwarded with her other mail from the old house. She'd thought about buying those shoes for Donte but decided against trying to dress him for obvious reasons.

The more Natasha stared at Henry, the more she had to admit she never quite liked him. He was a bald, short white man with hairy arms. He reminded her of an Italian butcher-slash-Mafia-member. She didn't know much about organized crime, but he looked like he had more Mafia ties than the entire Mob Wives cast. How could a woman trust a man that kept the top button of his shirt open, with strands of hair curling over the top of his tailored shirt for the entire world to see?

"How is that daughter of yours?" Henry asked, keeping up the small talk. "Nisha, right?"

He hoped that keeping their conversation light would soften the reality of their meeting. Before Shawn's death, Natasha had always seemed reserved and introverted; she let her husband do all of the decision-making. But these days, Natasha was voicing her own opinion, disagreeing on these terms, arguing that clause, etc. Henry had a feeling she'd absolutely have something to say about what he'd called her in for this time. He was about to drop another nuclear bomb from her husband's will, and neither of them would be comfortable.

"My daughter's name is Nivea," she corrected him. "And she is fine. Thank you for asking."

She noticed that Henry looked less settled than he normally did. He fidgeted with his hands as they walked, a body language display that meant uneasiness.

"Oh, I'm sorry," he apologized. "How unique. Did Mr. Winters come up with that?"

"Uh," Natasha hesitated, immediately becoming uncomfortable. "Mr. Wint—Shawn, he wasn't her birth father."

She cleared her throat. Now the conversation was going in

a completely different direction. Any talk about Nivea's father, Antonio, was off limits. She'd closed that door many years ago when she watched him hugged up with that white woman. She'd slammed it, as a matter of fact, and thrown away the key.

They approached Henry's office, not a moment too soon. His assistant, Stephanie, a young woman in her early 20s with a model build looked up from her desk.

"Stephanie, I will be in with Mrs. Winters for a moment. Please hold all calls," Henry announced.

Stephanie had beautiful, long hair and caramel skin. The smile she gave Natasha, however, was as fake as the lashes she wore. But the former First Lady understood. Women were always judging one another, especially in the African-American community. It was a fact Natasha had grown to accept. But she'd also learned early on that her job was not to condemn but to teach the young women coming behind her that it was not good practice. She'd started with teaching Nivea and her friends. And she would continue by not blaming this beautiful young woman for her actions. Natasha flashed Stephanie a genuine smile and decided that before she left the building, she'd find a way to say something nice to her.

Henry stood aside, allowing Natasha to pass before him. She hoped it wasn't for the reason of watching her walk away, but she let it slide and took a seat in front of his oversized desk.

"Henry, why am I here?" Natasha said as soon as he'd closed the door behind him.

"Would you like some coffee or water?" he responded.

She shifted in her seat. Did she look thirsty?

"No, Henry," she mentioned curtly, hoping that the shortness of her answer would cause him to skip to the reason for this meeting.

Natasha had a busy day ahead and didn't have time for anything that would keep her in this place longer than she wanted to be. She crossed her legs and placed her gloves neatly in her lap. As Henry moved to take a seat behind his desk, he noticed that she looked more powerful than he'd ever seen her. Her attire was the same, but she exuded a certain confidence he hadn't seen before.

"Mrs. Winters, I've called you here to inform you that your husband had another separate account that, um, we have to discuss," Henry began.

"Another one?" Natasha was less than thrilled to hear this news.

Henry looked down at the folder in front of him on his desk. He pulled out a printed contract before continuing.

"Normally, we disclose all details of the last will and testament at the first reading," Henry said, shuffling through the files. "But there was a clause for this particular addendum that ordered me to wait 180 days to disclose."

Natasha squinted in confusion. "I wasn't aware that people did that."

"Yes, one can make any changes they want to how their particular assets are distributed."

"Listen, Henry," Natasha felt heat rising up her neck as she waited for him to get to the point. "What do I have to sign? I just want to be done with this."

"Mrs. Winters," Henry started, sensing her frustration, "would you like some water before we proceed?"

"I've already told you, no water." Natasha could feel the irritation in her voice. She was holding it back with everything in her. "The details, Henry," she huffed at him.

"This separate account that Shawn Winters had contained three million dollars in it—" Henry folded the stapled page to show her the details.

Natasha stood up and grabbed the pages from him.

"Three million dollars?! What kind of joke is this?"

"There is no joke, Mrs. Winters," Henry responded. "The clause for your access to these funds reads that you must not marry within three years of his death."

"No, surely you are joking," Natasha responded frantically, reading the letters on the papers in her hands. A large lump was growing in her throat. With all the pressure involved in her situation with Donte, this new information didn't help any.

Natasha sat down again. She was sure that Henry was speaking to her, but she couldn't hear him over the pileup of her own thoughts. Her gloves had fallen to the floor in her previous outburst. With her free left hand, she rubbed her neck and then moved her manicured fingers to her temple. Natasha felt the urge to rise again, to pace as she formulated her next words. She was a calculated woman and didn't want to respond until she was ready. She suddenly found her left hand covering her mouth in an attempt to mask a scream she felt coming on.

"Mrs. Winters?"

Natasha looked up to see Henry's look of bewilderment and concern.

"Mrs. Winters," he said again, "I know that this is shocking, but I'm sure that there is a way that we can discuss this calmly."

It was as if Henry's words were hitting Natasha at a slower rate than they were leaving his mouth. Natasha looked around the room. Was she losing it? Three million dollars to remain a single, lonely, bitter widow? Who did Shawn think he was?

"...You know, discuss the details," Henry said. He held his hand out for the document still in her fingers' grasp, his eyes pleading with her to just remain calm.

In all honesty, Henry himself was speechless. He remembered seeing the beautiful and polished Natasha for the first time years ago. Shawn brought her in to sign a prenuptial agreement days before their wedding took place. In these past few months, he'd watched her endure more paperwork than any widow he'd ever represented in his career. He expected her to crumble months ago, but she hadn't. Even today, sitting in the chair with her head in her hand, there was something still ever so graceful about her.

"Please, Mrs. Winters, don't get upset. A beautiful woman like yourself shouldn't allow this to make you become…unraveled," Henry said, hoping a compliment would help the situation.

Henry had known Pastor Shawn for a number of years before the pastor hired him for legal counsel. Henry's wife, Sarai, and Natasha still attended Bible study together. Shawn was an emotionless man and never treated Natasha exceptionally well as a wife, but to do this to her, thought Henry, was wrong on more than one level. His opinion, however, didn't matter. The truth was, Shawn was one of his most affluent clients and Henry had always been well taken care of. Pastor Shawn may have been controlling, rude, and arrogant, but he was generous to those who worked for him. Three million could probably make any one happy—with or without a spouse.

Or maybe not. Pastor Shawn's Armor Bearer, Donte Smith, turned down Shawn's money when Henry explained the terms of the agreement to him. Shawn offered him a hefty $125,000 to leave

Atlanta and cease all contact with Natasha and her daughter. Henry barely had time to tell Mr. Smith that Shawn had also secured a position for him at a church in California before he got up and walked out of the office. He was angry, but he didn't say a word.

Apparently, Pastor Shawn had known since the day he'd married Nastahsa that Donte had loved her as well. Shawn also acknowledged that in his pain he'd asked Donte to take care of his wife, a request he'd regretted almost instantly. He'd been a fool; the thought of it was a debauchery to his position. And even if Donte was unlikely to take his money, $3 million was enough to secure his wife's agreement with the plan.

Henry remembered drafting that letter from Pastor Shawn that was now in Natasha's hands. She finally looked up at him.

"Henry," Natasha said at last. "My husband had a baby I never knew about, he lied to me about his health, and on top of that he controlled me until his dying day. I can't make a decision on this. Not today."

She placed the document back on Henry's desk, careful to be gentle. He would not see her completely lose her cool today. She been faithful to Shawn, and she had never given him a reason to believe that she was after his money. To do this to her was insulting, but she was a lady and would remain one.

"Is there anything else, Henry, I should know about my husband's final wishes before I go?" Natasha managed to slide through her clenched teeth.

Henry went on to tell her that, because of her refusal to sign immediately, a copy of the agreement would be mailed to her house in the next few days.

"Mrs. Winters, I know this is difficult for you," said Henry. "And I understand you needing time." He rose to walk her to the door. Natasha stood with him.

"Should you need additional legal counsel or just someone to talk to," Henry began, grabbing Natasha's gloves off the office floor, "Perhaps we could set up a time to have dinner."

The eyes of the Italian lawyer danced with the possibility that the widow might allow him to comfort her during her time of bereavement. It was something he'd wanted to do since he'd first seen her traveling behind the boisterous pastor; her submission was almost erotic. He loved the way the pencil skirt she wore today seemed to hug her waist and how her blouse clung to her breasts. They didn't seem as heavy as his wife's fake ones, but they still managed to capture his attention. Henry wondered in that moment what it was like to kiss a black woman. He walked closer to her and handed her back the pink gloves, his hands lingering on hers for a second too long.

"Either you are crazy or—." Natasha couldn't find the words. She snatched her hand from his.

"You are a disrespectful, foul little man," she said. "And furthermore, I'm not sure your wife—you know, Sarai—would approve of this apparent come-on to me." Natasha glared at Henry and pushed past him to let herself out.

She flung open the door, startling Stephanie.

"Stephanie," Natasha smiled, gathering herself instantly. "Your skin is positively radiant today. I meant to tell you that earlier."

Stephanie received the compliment gracefully, the gratitude shining in her brown eyes.

"Thank you, Mrs. Winters," she said.

"You're very welcome. Have a blessed day."

Natasha turned on her heels and marched toward the elevator, pressing the down button harder than she meant to. She could feel the tears rushing to her ducts, and she forced herself to keep it together. She definitely couldn't crumble with the receptionist looking on.

The time it took for her to ride the elevator down to the lobby and make her way out the front doors of the building seemed like an eternity. As Natasha walked through the parking lot, she couldn't help but feel she was being watched. If Shawn would place that kind of condition on her that she'd just read, he'd probably also gone to extreme measures to have her life on full surveillance.

Natasha slid into the driver's seat of her car and slammed the door. For all she knew, her Mercedes was bugged too. She started the engine and pulled out of the lot to head back to her house. As she drove, she felt the pent-up tears running down the sides of her face. She quickly wiped them away with her left hand and placed it back on the steering wheel. She looked down at her now bare finger. The imprint of the wedding ring Shawn had given her was beginning to fade. The 5-carat beauty was sitting in her nightstand, right next to the equally beautiful one Donte gave her when he asked for her hand.

Her eyes on the road were useless now with all the tears getting in the way. Natasha pulled into a nearby gas station and parked her car. She wanted nothing more than to feel the embrace of a man who loved her after the morning she'd had.

Natasha pressed the speakerphone button on her steering wheel.

"Call Donte."

"Call Friar. Is this correct?" the voice-activated feature incorrectly iterated back to her.

"No," she sniffled. "Call Donte."

"Call Darren. Is this correct?"

"No," she began screaming. "No. No. No. No. No. Call Donte."

Natasha realized her words were inaudible over her sobs. She held her hands to her tearstained face and rested her head on her steering wheel. The weight of the morning fell on her, and she realized not even Donte could save her in this moment.

"God, why did you have to choose me?" she whispered through her tears. She began beating her dashboard senselessly as her sadness turned into rage.

She had lost 10 pounds since burying Shawn, all of it stress-related. Instead of holding up the household like she was accustomed to doing, Natasha was now leaning on Nivea more than ever for support in these trying times. A good day for her was one in which she actually left her house, which was usually only for church and Bible study with Donte or for a Deborah's Daughters meeting. Bad days were spent on her sofa watching the television network, OWN. Worse days were spent with her face in her pillow.

Less overwhelmed than before, Natasha began to tell God about the loneliness she felt. She told God it wasn't just the intimacy but the feeling of being protected that she missed most.

"Why did you choose me to feel this pain," she cried to the Lord. "To endure this hurt. He's gone and now I don't know what to do."

Natasha unleashed all the frustrations, all the pain of it to God. She knew that from the outside of the car she must have looked crazy, but she had been holding this in for so long, she simply couldn't take it anymore. Since the funeral and the proposal, she had just closed herself off to the outside world. And furthermore, she had begun closing herself off to Donte. Sure, he still came by for dinner and picked them up for church, but her suspended answer hung over them like a cloud. It made things awkward, Natasha admitted. She wished that there was a widow's handbook so that she would know how to act after losing a husband.

She felt lost. She felt alone. But more than anything, she felt betrayed.

"It hurts so bad, Lord," Natasha said, exasperated. "Some days, I hate you for it."

With those words, she stayed silent, sitting in the midst of her rage and hurt. Clearly, the countless hours of bereavement counseling—one of the stipulations that Shawn had made mandatory in his will—weren't helping. It was only to preserve his reputation, just like forbidding her to remarry was.

"Reputation," she laughed to herself.

She wondered why she should even care about what a bunch of hypocrites thought anyway. The visits from her members were far and few in-between these days. Two months after the funeral, they sent her a check inside of a blank card without so much as a signature from the interim pastor. And that was it. They had nothing else to say to her, but they found the words to whisper amongst themselves when she shared a Bible with Donte on Thursdays and Sundays.

"Reputation," Natasha repeated to herself. "Oh, Shawn."

She began to tear up again. It was clear she would have to fully close the door on her past before she could even think about moving forward. Reaching into her purse, she retrieved her cell phone and dialed Donte's number.

"Hey Tash," Donte answered.

"Hey."

"Are you alright? Where are you?" Donte asked, sensing something was wrong.

"I'm good. I'm on my way home," Natasha responded. "We need to talk. Can you meet me there?"

AMAURI

"Knock knock."

Amauri stood at the doorway of Paden's office, peeking into his domain. Her husband was busy at his iMac, typing away. "Paden, I hate to interrupt you, but I was wondering if you and I could talk about Grace's birthday party."

Grace, their oldest child, was turning three years old. Amauri figured that with their youngest, Cammy, crawling around the house now, her big girl was feeling a little neglected.

"I want to do something special for her with all her friends before we leave town," she finished, walking into the room.

"I'm ok with that," answered Bishop Paden, his eyes never leaving his desktop.

Amauri was sure that he was making the final changes on a book he'd been writing, but she couldn't let him forget that before there was a ministry there was her. In fact, her motive for bothering him this early in the morning had less to do with Grace's birthday and more to do with her wanting to close the apparent gap between them that had grown over the past six months.

It all began when she'd snuck off to New York to visit her attacker, the one that had almost killed her, in prison. She didn't tell anyone she was going, not even Paden. The day that she had given her testimony and restored the relationship between Lynette and her husband, she'd spilled how she had the courage to look her attacker in the face and tell him she forgave him. It was one of the hardest things she'd ever done, but it had healed her, restored her, and now she was finally able to move forward.

Bishop Paden, however, was furious. He'd scolded her as if she was a child and interrogated her to the point where she felt as if she'd done something wrong. He'd made her replay the scene over and over.

It was simple. She'd sat down in front of her assailant, Montez, her heart beating through her ears. She found herself ranting emotionally for a few minutes until she had a chance to come up for air. He just sat there staring at her silently while she sobbed. In the end, she looked at him and knew in her heart that God had given her peace about it all.

I want you to know that I forgive you. Those were the last words she said to him.

Montez just got up from the chair he was sitting in, shook his head, and called for the guard to take him back to his cell.

Amauri hadn't expected for him to apologize. Forgiveness, to her, wasn't about his response; it was about her response to God. The Lord had done far too many great things in her life for her to be harboring ill will for anyone. After a day or two, Bishop Paden apologized to her for becoming so upset, but she could tell that he still felt uneasy about what she'd done.

"You remember that one party we went to for Sister Ingrid's daughter?" Amauri asked, trying to get Paden's attention again. "I want to ask her where she got all those princess decorations from."

"Sweetheart, I can't really focus on that right now," Bishop Paden responded, still refusing to tear his eyes away from the screen. "But if you give me about 30 minutes, I will be upstairs and we can go over every detail of this fairytale party. Ok?"

Bishop Paden was emailing a group of New York pastors in preparation for their move. He didn't want to bring up anything that involved New York around Amauri. Since they'd made the big decision to move, she'd seemed upset. He knew that the next few months were going to be hard—extremely so—but they decided a long time ago that if they were going to allow God to use them as vessels, then they had to make the hard decisions together.

"I talked to the ladies today about the going way party," Amauri tried again. "I'm excited! What about you?"

"Yea, sweetheart. Excited."

"Paden, honey," Amauri whined from her spot in the doorway. "What's wrong?"

"Nothing, love," Bishop Paden said, finally looking up at her. "I'm just working on a lot right now."

"Are you sure?" she asked, her eyes meeting his.

"I'm sure," Bishop Paden answered, returning to the keyboard in front of him.

The truth was, Paden was hiding something. He knew a truth that could shatter his marriage, but he wasn't ready to share just yet. He wasn't ready to almost lose the woman that had changed his life. She had given him two beautiful babies and a life that he only dreamed of when he was trapped in his other life. Bishop Paden had tried his hardest to keep that life from her, to protect her. He loved his wife and loved how God was healing her. He wouldn't be responsible for setting her back in any way.

Amauri frowned at her husband's response. Lately, Bishop Paden had been so caught up with the activities of the church that their lives had become something like a drive-thru. Bishop Paden was only home for a few hours at a time, then it was off to this meeting, that impact group, etc. Was Amauri jealous? Maybe. She recalled the stories that Shenae shared of her ex-husband's full plate. Leon had almost missed the last years of their children's time in high school. Amauri rebuked the thought instantly; she trusted her husband and would not compare him to the traitor that Leon had become in the end to Shenae.

Overwhelmed by the need for her husband, Amauri decided she wouldn't leave just yet. She carefully closed the door behind her and tiptoed further into the room toward her husband. He continued tapping away at his desk, unaware that she hadn't left the room.

"Paden," Amauri called for her husband.

"Yea," Bishop Paden answered, a little startled.

"Look at me."

Bishop Paden swiveled around in his office chair to find Amauri standing before him. Her feet were bare and she wore the cutoff shorts he liked so much. Fitting like a glove on her upper body was a T-shirt that Bishop Paden had bought for her. "Fearfully made for him," it read, hugging her breasts ever so well.

"Nan is with the girls upstairs," Amauri whispered. "I want some attention."

She wanted to remind him that, at the end of the day, after he'd shaken the new members' hands and hung his robe, there were two little girls and a wife that needed him. Her eyes were saying, P, it's time for a break.

"P-love, I need you," she continued, her voice sultry and low, reminding him that although she wore the title of a First Lady, she also knew how to keep her husband happy and intimately satisfied. It was more than praying for him and attending to his everyday needs; he also needed the secret, sexy time that only his wife could give him.

"Really?" he responded in amusement, the dimple in his right cheek gleaming at her, giving her permission to get closer and pursue the object of her affection. "What can I help you with, Mrs. Paden?"

Amauri proceeded to move closer to him, swaying her hips right and left as she walked. Bishop Paden sat back against the cool leather chair as his wife straddled him. She removed his glasses and threw them on the desk behind him. He then grabbed a handful of her blonde tresses and pulled her towards him into a searing kiss. As he allowed his tongue to dance with hers, she pushed herself against him. Impatient, Amauri reached into his sweatpants and gripped her husband's manhood. He was rock hard in her hands.

"Ooh," she smiled at him, biting her lips in anticipation of the pleasure to come. "Is that a gavel in your pants, Judge Paden?"

"Why don't you find out for yourself?" he asked her.

Taking her time, she got up and pulled down his sweats. Paden's eyes were motionless on Amauri, his stone cold gaze unaffected by her probing. Moving to her knees and licking the inside of her palm, she grabbed him in her hands, allowing the heat to fuse with the silkiness of his skin. She looked up and saw the beginning of his unravel. She perched between his legs and soaked him with her mouth, refusing to be neat. He liked the sound. Amauri slid her hands up and down, teasing it with kisses and licks before taking him all in. Paden was getting lost in the pleasure of it all. His words of gratitude were broken, choppy, and incoherent. He wanted to grab her blonde locks but decided against it for fear that she'd retreat.

"Babe, it's ok. Touch me," she said, reading his mind.

It was more of a plea than a command. She was so much more comfortable in her skin, and it made him so proud. He wasted no time in running his fingers through her hair, his eyes locked on the sky to keep calm.

"Look at me," she whispered.

He attempted to oblige her and nearly lost it. Piqued with his loss of control, he stood her up and turned her away from him. Pulling her onto his lap, he placed soft kisses on her back and the nape of her neck. He unbuckled the button of her shorts, a nuisance against his gropes. Sliding his hands through the silk string, Paden found the treasure of her wetness.

Amauri moaned in passion as he skillfully circled the peak of her crest in his fingers, pushing her towards her edge. Her legs nearly buckled as he grabbed her tiny waist in his arms and slipped her onto his waiting member. She rode in sync with him, her breathing quickening, her moans coming more ravenous and sexy. The strangled sounds of her climax nearly threatened to cause him to cum again.

Effortlessly, he lifted his tiny wife to face him. In one swift motion, Paden had her in his arms, her legs wrapped around his 6'4" stature. He carried her to the leather couch on the other side of his office, amidst the array of pictures of him and prominent pastors, the various accolades and certifications. This moment was perfect; he could finally get his mind off everything. As he laid her down, his lips grazed her cheeks first. Purposely missing her lips to build her anticipation, he planted kisses to her forehead, chin, and neck. There, his mouth was met with a soft grumble of frustration vibrating from Amauri's throat.

He laughed to himself and gently grabbed his wife's face with one hand.

"I love you," he told her.

"I love you too, P," she told him.

Staring down at his wife of more than 12 years, Paden had to admit that she still turned him on. She was so spontaneous, and ever since she allowed herself to be healed from the mental anguish of her attack, he was staring at a whole woman.

With that, she kissed him tenderly, getting lost in him. She was anxious to complete their moment. He loved watching her like this, impatient and desirous.

"Let me get on top," Amauri breathed at him.

He smiled at her in delight and gave her permission. She clutched him, and with her own strength, she flipped herself to straddle him. Paden pulled her shirt above her head and gazed up at her beautiful breasts response to freedom. He began to stroke her nipples with his fingers as she slid onto him easily. There, she would create their magic. Her body just moved, singing to him with its rhythm. His hands clutched her waist as he met her with each slippery stroke. Her delicate arms pushed against his chest. She was trembling now, losing control. There was nothing in the world that compared to how they shared each other. They never tired or grew bored with their lovemaking. They were both open to being more inventive now that they had two little girls around. Amauri was determined that she wouldn't let herself become secondary to her husband's title.

Biting her lip as the waves of pleasure ran through her, she took her time and let him feel all of her. His fingers moved to graze the scars on her body that once held her hostage. He couldn't take his eyes off her; the woman that three years ago couldn't make love to him with the lights on was now performing for him with the noonday sun beaming in.

She was his angel; she'd saved him when all he thought he had was God. He couldn't keep himself from giving in any longer. Am-auri felt his release and collapsed on top of him.

"You a bad girl, Mrs. Paden."

Breathlessly laughing, his satisfied wife whispered back, "You better not forget it."

SHENAE

"Mom, have you talked to Dad?" Shawn asked.

"No, Shawn, I haven't," Shenae responded from the other end of the line. She stood on her tiptoes with the receiver wedged between her ear and shoulder so she could use both hands. Her main task at the moment was grabbing a box marked "Old Life" from the garage.

"Please tell Leon to stop calling me," she added, a bit irritated now that her soon-to-be ex-husband had been brought into the conversation.

Shenae reached again for the box with no luck. She remembered telling Shawn to put it there before he left for the semester—out of sight, out of mind. But, of course, today she absolutely needed something that could only be in that forsaken box.

"Shawn, hold on," Shenae told her son, placing the phone on the bottom shelf.

She reached up once more, stretching her slender frame to its extent. Still, no luck.

"Ugh, forget it," Shenae decided, picking up the phone. It was times like these that she wished she had a man around the house. Her sons Shawn and Samuel were both away at their respective colleges, so there was a lengthy period of time where anything that was beyond her arm's span would remain there until they returned for a break or holiday.

"Hello?"

"Really, Mom? Leon. That's a bit harsh," Shawn responded to his mother's insistence to never utter her husband's nickname again.

"It is your father's name."

"You never call him that," said Shawn. Shenae could sense that he was taken aback. She thought to retaliate but decided against it. She wouldn't involve him with any battles, internally or otherwise, that she was having with Shawn. She stayed quiet, resting against her car in the garage.

"You have to forgive him, Mom," Shenae finally heard him say.

She smiled and decided to change the subject. "Boo-Bear, this is not up for discussion. How are you? How is seminary going?"

"It's so hard, Mom. Plus, New York is such a strange place and it's insanely lonely."

"You just make sure that you focus on your schoolwork. You know Bishop Paden is moving back there, though. That'll be nice to spend some time with him when he gets there."

"That'll be cool. I'd have somebody here that I know besides my brother. People get us confused all the time here, Ma," Shawn laughed. "We are nothing alike. Sam's a dancer."

"Though your gifts are different, son," Shenae scolded, "you are alike in more ways than you know. Don't be so hard on him."

"Mom, he's different."

"Hey," Shenae said a little firmer. "God loves the man and hates the sin. Now, let's move on."

"So, you're telling me that we are not going to address this?"

"Address this on your knees and let God do what he is going to do," Shenae answered. She was desperately trying to avoid any more conversation with her son about Samuel's alternate lifestyle.

"Fine. But he told me that he signed you up for E-Fish.com…"

Oh no, Shenae thought. She wasn't prepared for this topic either.

"What's up with that? You trying to get a man?" Shawn pushed.

"Shawn, that is not any of your business."

"Because Dad," he started to tell her the news his father dropped the other day, "he told me that he—."

"I said already that I don't want to discuss your father," Shenae cut him off. "Look, I think I hear the mailman outside. I'll call you later, sweetie."

Shenae hung up and hit the garage door opener. She knew she was being evasive as ever with her son, but there were just some things she wasn't ready to talk about. And yes, she'd signed up for E-Fish, an online Christian dating site, on a lonely whim. She'd called Samuel because she was clueless as to how to even set up the profile. Ten minutes into the process, she felt desperate and alone and signed off. She'd only been on the site a few times since then, but how do you explain a dating profile to a young man who still hopes his parents can rekindle the flame?

And how could she ever go back to Leon? He had deceived her and stolen her life. All that she'd envisioned for her life's plan was gone in the blink of an eye. It'd been over a year since she'd left him, but the sting of his betrayal was still fresh. And everyone—except Shenae—kept trying to revisit that wound.

Shenae gave her mailman a wave as he drove by. Walking to the mailbox, a fresh aggravation fell onto her shoulders. She instantly flashed back to the night that she had last seen Leon in person. He was set to be sentenced the next day and, for some reason, Shenae decided to go and see him. The truth was, she was overwhelmed with grief. In her pain, she and Leon ended up involved in a rather sad attempt at lovemaking. To Shenae, it solidified that, in both her heart and her body, their marriage was truly over. She remembered fleeing the house in tears afterward, convinced that though they were still married legally, they couldn't be further away from each other in the flesh.

She shook it off and opened her mailbox. Bills, bills, magazines for the boys, and a letter from Leon-the-Incarcerated.

"Are you kidding me?" Shenae muttered.

She was two seconds from ripping it up but thought that perhaps it had something to do with her lawyer's visit to Leon last week. Shenae ripped it open and read its contents from her driveway.

"Due to good behavior, my sentence has been reduced..." Shenae felt the words come out of her mouth like hot ash.

I'll see you soon, Shenae. Love, Lee

Shenae stood fuming as she crumpled the letter between her fingers.

"Crap!" she hollered out in pain, looking down at the fingernail she nearly lost in the midst of her anger.

How ironic, though, that she'd rather have a splitting paper cut than break one of her fingernails. A woman on a budget hated a broken nail as much as an unexpected bill—or an estranged husband getting out of jail early. She walked back to her house thinking, Who knew a routine walk to the mailbox could throw a woman's entire day off?

She reached her house nauseous and anxious to get inside. A classy woman such as herself would reserve a breakdown for the comfort of her home. As soon as she let down the garage door behind her, Shenae bolted for the porcelain bowl in the guest bathroom downstairs. There, she felt her morning oatmeal forcing itself back up.

"This can't be real," Shenae moaned as she sat on the floor under the window by the toilet. "It must be some kind of mistake."

She wasn't ready to face him yet. God knew she wasn't ready to see Leon. A bead of sweat seemed to break through the chills and began to slide down the center of her back. Could this be the news that the twins had been trying to tell her a few weeks ago over the phone? Any time anyone tried to bring up anything Leon, Shenae immediately checked out. But the fact was, he was still their twins' father. He'd disappointed everyone in the world with his deceit, but the kids still saw him as their father. He'd been a good provider for his family, and as much as Shenae refused to admit it, Sam needed a strong male figure now more than ever.

Her new Persian cat, Sasha, peered into the bathroom. Sasha had been an impulse buy to curb the loneliness. A random visit to the pound one afternoon led to a new member of her family. Living in solitary had been almost miserable for Shenae. Immersing herself in the prayer calls and outreach program were not enough to fill the gaping hole of a missing spouse. If anything, it had intensified her desire to share the ministry moments with someone.

Almost immediately, Shenae realized that she missed being married. She laid her head against the wall behind her and cursed herself for opening the letter in the first place. She had done well thus far, ignoring all calls and refusing to write him. Usually, Leon's letters were dripping with romance and obscenities detailing how much he missed her. She only allowed them because she badly hoped that he would finally take responsibility for his actions. It was as if he didn't realize he was in prison; perhaps he thought this was some Pastor's retreat and that his wife wasn't divorcing him.

"Ugh," Shenae groaned, pulling her knees closer to her.

Divorce was such an ugly word. The fresh pain of losing her marriage to her husband's infidelity and constant deception crept into her thoughts. Sasha now joined her, rubbing against her legs, looking at her for affection.

"Who am I going to rub against to get some affection? Hmm?" Shenae asked her pet, stroking its fur.

She felt a wind of sadness follow that rhetorical question. She was so angry with Leon that she could barely breathe. She began to pray, her left hand still on Sasha, her right hand lifted to the heavens. Slow tears began to build as she cried out to God, her only refuge during these trying months of pain. Suddenly, she heard the familiar siren from her computer telling her that she had received a message.

"Amen," Shenae finished, wiping her tears and staggering to her computer desk.

She sat down in her overpriced, plush leather chair, immediately thankful that she'd splurged on this particular item. Since the divorce and the freezing of her assets, she had been budgeting out of control. But, she had decided to spend a little extra for the chair. Shenae remembered seeing it in her favorite consignment shop. The items there reminded her that the best treasures were the ones that others discarded. This chair represented that no matter what she went through, her greatest gift in life was her own self. She was valuable, even if Leon hadn't seen it. And she knew that when God did send someone, that man would see how amazing she was. She felt Sasha against her legs again and thanked God for bringing her immediate comfort.

Tapping her mouse to awaken her computer, Shenae found that she had a message on E-Fish.com. She had a few winks too, which Sam had told her meant that men were interested in her.

"Winks," she said aloud to herself with a laugh. The world had truly changed since the last time she dated. She'd met Leon the old-fashioned way and he courted her. She still appreciated a handwritten note and face-to-face encounters. Now, men sent winks and messages through the computer. But, she had to admit, the Internet seemed like a semi-safe place to meet someone. And with all the attention she was getting, Shenae felt like she was ready to explore the options.

FROM: Souledout81

SUBJECT: Hey there…

Shenae had to read the message twice, but it looked as if she was being asked out on a date. Souledout81, whose real name was Angelo, was one of her frequent IM friends who also happened to be 13 years her junior. They had been casually chatting back and forth for about a month. Sure, they seemed to get along great via the Internet, but the prospect of meeting this stranger in person was slightly disturbing. Before she realized it, she'd convinced herself to reply.

FROM: Shenae84554

SUBJECT: RE: Hey there...

Shenae's hands were moving rapidly, typing that she'd love to have coffee after her Deborah's Daughter meeting today. She pressed send and felt like a 17-year-old girl who'd just accepted a date to prom.

Wait, what did this Angelo even look like? She frantically searched through his profile for his picture but came up empty. So, he knew what she looked like, but she'd be going in blind. She laughed. What had she gotten herself into?

As the phone rang, interrupting her thoughts, Shenae decided that after coffee, she'd let her pursuer down easy. This was silly. She didn't want to end up on the E-Fish commercials as they chronicled her dating life.

She looked at the caller ID: Fulton County Penitentiary. As if this wasn't enough of a jam-packed day, of course Leon was calling her. "Hello?" she answered. "Yes, I'll accept the charges."

LYNETTE

"Dre!" Lynette called out. She was running frantically up the tall staircase leading to their bedroom. She knew he'd be in there studying or relaxing.

"Hey, baby, what's up?" Pastor Andre ran out of the bedroom, matching her intensity, and met her at the top of the stairs. Lynette saw him press END on his cell phone and slip the device into his trousers. She thought to ask him who he had just been talking to, but her instinct told her they'd come too far to go back because of her assumptions.

"I just wanted to say, I love you," she giggled instead, tossing the desire to probe about the call.

Lynette had found a new love for her husband. He constantly reminded her why she became his wife so many years ago. The pain of their past problems had long disappeared, and whenever Lynette found herself thinking about it, she openly talked to her husband and they prayed together.

"You are so silly," he said with a kiss. "I love you back, woman. That was Bishop Paden on the phone. He needs to see me today and go over some things."

Andre pulled her closer and showered his wife with playful kisses until she began to laugh uncontrollably.

"Ew!!" yelled their two children, Benny and Ivory, peering out of their playroom.

"You can't kiss Mom in the hallway," Benny yelled, running toward his father.

"Well, why don't I steal your kisses?" Lynette said, scooping Benny in her arms. She spun him around and began to furiously tickle him.

Pastor Andre could sense the jealousy of his pint-sized Ivory, who was now a little older than 18 months. He picked her up and began to assault her with kisses just as he had done her mother moments earlier.

After demanding a truce, the rambunctious children ran back into their playroom together. It was Lynette's favorite sound these days, the overzealous conversations of her little ones. She took a moment to stare at their father, who was catching his breath from all the action. She felt like a teenager watching him. Even after the heartbreak they had survived, she still found him sexy; she was in love with everything about him, from his perfect white teeth to the cleft of his chin.

Pastor Andre caught his wife eyeing him and smiled.

"Are you enjoying the show, First Lady?" he asked.

"I was about to enjoy it more than you know," she responded, closing the gap between them and taking his lips in a kiss.

"Beautiful, I'd love to," Pastor Andre started, "but I have meetings today and so do you."

Lynette whined in defeat. He was right; they had more responsibilities now than ever before. As the newly ordained senior pastors of Promised Land Ministries, there was always much work to be done. They hadn't had time to play as often as she liked these days. Sometimes, Lynette just wanted to steal her husband away and get lost in him. But, duty called, and she loved her new responsibility as the Church Events Coordinator. It gave her the opportunity to express her creative side while also watching their new ministry grow.

"Fine," Lynette sighed. "I guess I'll go get ready then."

She brushed past him to make her way to the bedroom. Andre, undecided as to whether he would follow his own advice, grabbed Lynette's arm before she passed. He pulled his wife close and pressed himself into her. Kissing her there, Andre he took the liberty of running his hands up and down Lynette's new, fuller frame.

"These curves are going to get me into trouble," he whispered into her ear.

"The Word reminds us that you must enjoy the wife of your youth," Lynette smirked. "When was the last time you did that?"

Pastor Andre smiled. He knew he had been neglecting her, but it wasn't intentional. With Bishop Paden leaving for New York soon, his schedule had gone from zero to crazy.

"Babe, go get ready," said Andre, pulling away from Lynette. "I have to head down to the church and meet Bishop."

Lynette kissed his neck in response. Andre could feel himself getting excited at her touch. So much had changed between them, but one thing was certain and unfaltering. They carried a passion and fire for each other unlike anything either had experienced since they first said their nuptials.

"You sure?" she asked, kissing him again.

"I was two seconds ago," he said, allowing her passionate pecking to continue.

It wasn't the physical intimacy that satisfied him so much as it was the fact that his wife was openly sharing herself with him at last. So much good had come out of all the bad that had occurred. When Lynette's father, Frank, lost his wife, she invited him to come live in Atlanta to start fresh. Pastor Andre knew that having him there for the birth of their daughter meant so much to Lynette. And now that he was there full-time for both his grandchildren and for his daughter, it was as if his wife was reaping all the benefits of true forgiveness.

"Go, Lynn," Pastor Andre pulled away from her once more. "I'll watch Benny and Ivory."

He kissed his gorgeous wife's hands before turning her toward the bedroom, stealing glances as she walked away from him.

"I know you're looking at my booty," Lynette giggled over her shoulder.

"It's mine," he responded. "I'll look if I want."

Pastor Andre's cell phone violently ringing in his pocket interrupted his trance. The number was unknown, so he answered with hesitation.

"Hello? This is Pastor Andre."

"Hi, Pastor Andre," answered a frenzied yet familiar voice on the other end. "This is Harriet. Can you talk?"

"Harriet?"

Hearing the name of the woman that once ruined her life, Lynn turned around to see her husband's face grow bright red. Pastor Andre's eyes met hers as he answered.

"Harriet," he said again, more calmly now. "What can I do for you?"

Lynette felt a queasiness wave over her. She wanted to rush him and grab the phone and rip Harriet a new one. How dare she call him after all she'd put their family through? She watched Pastor Andre down the hall, bracing himself against the wall rubbing the back of his head in defeat.

"What do you mean?" she heard him ask in a stressed tone.

Lynette's eyes darted toward their children's playroom. Pastor Andre took the hint and lowered his voice.

"Yea…Ok…Ok, Fine," was all she could make out now. "Look, we'll take care of it later. Goodbye."

When Pastor Andre hung up the phone, he looked as sick as Lynette felt.

"What was that all about?" Lynette said, rushing to grab her husband's face. He wasn't speaking yet, but his eyes told her that it was something big.

"Why would she even call here? The nerve of that tri—."

"Lynn," Pastor Andre stopped her.

"Sorry," she apologized. Lynette almost returned to a place she'd been delivered from.

"Harriet...um," he stammered.

"What about her, honey?" Lynn said, trying to be calm and soothing as she could see her husband losing it. Pastor Andre slid down the wall onto the floor and hid his face from her.

"Her husband found out about...us," Pastor Andre said, trying to find the words. "He asked for a DNA test on their son."

Lynette considered what he'd just admitted. She remembered Harriet's son; he had to be at least four years old now.

"It wasn't his," Lynette found herself saying aloud.

She fought back tears as Pastor Andre shook his head.

"They want to do a second test on me," he said, finally looking up at Lynette. "They think I may be the father."

They sat in silence for moments at those words. Both sat on the floor staring up at God, wondering what He could possibly be teaching them with this newest test.

Lynette began to pray.

"Father, in the name of Jesus, You see our lives and You see what is happening," she started, grabbing her husband's hand. "Now, God, I pray for my husband to find peace in whatever your decision is. Father, I pray that our marriage stays strong as we yield and depend on you."

The First Lady went into prayer, because at that moment she knew that her husband needed to know that she wasn't going anywhere. They had worked so hard to get to this place, and she wasn't about to let the enemy's distraction intervene with what God was building in their relationship and ministry.

"Hey, you listen to me," she said once she'd finished. "We will get through anything."

She kissed his tears of self-disappointment away.

"I am not going anywhere, baby. Come on." Lynette stood up and held her hands out to pull her husband off the floor.

"I love you, babe," Pastor Andre said to his wife. He felt more confident and assured than before.

"Love you too. Watch the kids until the sitter gets here. I'm going to go get ready." Lynette turned and walked to their bedroom. Closing the door behind her, an onset of tears met her immediately. She ran to the bathroom to run the water to mask her sobs.

"Oh, God," she cried at the edge of the tub.

Forgiveness didn't mean that everything would go back to normal. But she wished this all would just go away. More than anything, she wanted them to rebuild their lives together. Every day, she was reminded of her husband's indiscretion. And now, she would have to deal with the possibility that he fathered a child with the woman that almost destroyed them.

NATASHA

Donte stood at the front door of Natasha's house, waiting for her to answer. It seemed like he was always waiting on her, ever since he'd proposed months ago. His intention today was to tell her that he would no longer run to her beckoning call. She had been treating him like a stand-in father figure and a pretend boyfriend.

But all that went out the door when Donte saw her. She stood in the entrance to her house, looking like she'd been through a shipwreck morning. She still glowed to him, though. Her curls were down, framing her round face. He could see the crease from where it had been in a bun. Clearly, she'd just pulled it out and let it be as reckless as she felt. Natasha was wearing one of his jerseys that he'd left over her house. She was wearing her reading glasses, barely hiding her makeup stained face. He wanted to laugh at how pitiful she looked, but honestly, she looked irresistible.

"Tash, what's wrong?" he asked, rushing in and scooping her in his strong arms. "You only wear your glasses after a good cry."

He'd prepped himself to tell her that he wasn't going to wait forever and she came to the door and made him remember all the things he loved about her. He hugged her tighter. His embrace broke the trance Natasha had been in.

"Hey," she hugged him back. "Thanks for coming."

Donte let her go and she stepped to the side to let him into the foyer. His scent greeted Natasha, causing her to close her eyes in appreciation. There was nothing more intoxicating than the enticing smell of a man. Natasha looked up at Donte, a bit overwhelmed by how masculine he really was. It had to be a sin to smell that good and look that good in a pair of jeans. Natasha tried to chastise her wayward mind but instead allowed herself a moment to allow Donte's presence to be felt. She may have been a woman with a dead husband, but no part of her body was dead at that moment. Donte's broad shoulders just looked like they needed something to hold up. His muscles filled that hideous Hawaiian shirt so well. His hair was cut close to his head, and his goatee rounded his chocolate face perfectly. She wondered how many minutes he spent trimming it.

"So, why did you want me to rush over here?" Donte asked, making his way into the living room to sit down. "Natasha?"

Jarring herself back to reality, she felt a warm flush of embarrassment. Natasha Winters had lusted for a man for almost half a minute. She thought about how many feathers she would lose in her wings for those thoughts she just had.

"Listen, we need to talk about what you asked me," Natasha explained.

Donte looked at her. Natasha was rubbing her palms together as she spoke, and if he knew her like he thought he did, she'd start pacing soon enough. She was obviously nervous. Even though she put up the exterior that she was hard as a rock, he knew she wasn't. Life had taught her not to trust men, and Pastor Shawn had made it clear why she shouldn't. But Donte wanted to prove to her that he was different.

"First, let me say this," Donte interrupted her before she could say another word. "I asked you to be my wife, Natasha. I asked you to be the woman that I wake up to each day. I asked you to let me be the last man that makes love to you."

He motioned for her to have a seat beside him on the couch before continuing.

"Don't treat my proposal like I asked you to go have a burger with me," he stressed, holding her hands in his. "I watched you marry a man that I knew wasn't for you. And now I'm asking you to marry one that you and I both know is absolutely for you."

He smiled at her, hoping she could hear the sincerity ringing from his heart. This wasn't the first time that Donte had been extremely open with her. But he hoped that this time she would actually hear him. He slid his hands up Natasha's arms, leaving his thumbs in the crease of her elbow. Natasha tried not to melt in that moment. Donte's touch was comforting; his words were nourishing the brokenness inside of her.

"I have watched you over this past year attempting to pick up the pieces of your life," he continued. "Instead of coming closer to the one that could help you, you've torn yourself away from me, Natasha. You've allowed the opinions of others to be the reason that we are not together."

He was right. She'd consulted her fellow Deborah's Daughters on one occasion; each gave her their version as to why she shouldn't marry Donte. She listened to the gossiping tongues at church, the congregation that was probably glad to be rid of her as a First Lady. But what did she want? What did Natasha want?

"I will never love anyone more than I love you," Donte pleaded. "I need you to hear me. I will never love another woman the way that I love you."

He moved closer to her. He was now in her personal space, a bubble that was off-limits for a woman who'd recently been made a widow. Natasha tried to look away, but his massive hands softly turned her face towards his. His brown eyes told her that he meant everything he said to her.

"I love you Natasha," he said. "Do you know that?"

Natasha knew that he would love and take care of her, but she had to think logically. Donte was right; this was not simply a burger run. This was a major decision that would affect her for the rest of her life. Nivea needed a father figure, yes, but did she really need a new father?

With his other hand, Donte intertwined his fingers with hers. Natasha knew what was coming now. She felt the closeness and the tension between them growing. She was about to experience her first kiss with this man, who loved her and cherished her.

"Do you know I love you, Natasha?" he asked again.

"Yes," she whispered, nose-to-nose with him now.

He sealed her confession with a kiss. It was gentle, loving, and dreamy. Natasha felt the desire to faint against him, only because she knew he'd be there to catch her as he had for so long now.

His hand cupped her face and his thumb traced her cheek as he kissed her again. He didn't probe her mouth open with his or stir embers inside her that he knew they couldn't extinguish yet. But she felt his passion, nonetheless.

"Donte, I can't do this right now," she said, breaking the kiss. "Things are just so complicated."

She refused to look at him and stared at the ground instead. That wasn't what she meant to say. Natasha wanted to tell him that she, too, was falling in love with him. But she wanted to make sure she wasn't fragile when she said it.

"Ok," she heard him say with a heavy sigh. "I'll keep waiting then. I'll wait for you to realize what I already know."

Donte put one hand to his head and sighed again.

"But let me be clear," he said to her, standing up. "I will not stand around and watch another man court you…if that's what this is about."

Natasha looked up, confused. He was serious.

"I promise this is not about any other man," she said, standing up to embrace him. "I just need to figure out what I really want and find healing for the issues that I've had over the past year."

So much had taken place, but she knew she couldn't use that as an excuse for much longer.

"I'm really having a hard time with how everything is playing out," Natasha continued. "And I don't want to confuse it by having you in my bed—."

She cupped her mouth at her Freudian slip.

"I meant head," she corrected herself.

They both chuckled.

"You haven't eaten all day," said Donte, changing the subject by reading her mind. "I'll make you something to eat. Stuffed ravioli sound good?"

He turned and walked into the kitchen. Natasha followed him, grateful to have him in her life. He was such a good friend to her. She watched him pull a pot out and begin to boil some water. In response, she grabbed the pre-stuffed pasta from the freezer and the sauce from her pantry.

"I wish I could just abandon my reservations, you know?" she admitted to him as his back was turned. "And just fall for you the way I want to."

"What's stopping you?" he asked her, searching for something in the cabinet.

"I don't know," she began to lie. "I mean, I can't just go around dating men that used to serve my husband in ministry."

"Ex-husband," he reminded her.

"You know what I mean," Natasha snapped back at him.

"No," he said calmly. "I don't. You're reading so much into this that you are forgetting to let God lead you."

Natasha instantly wished she hadn't brought the topic up at all again.

"I don't hear God right now," she said softly.

"Well that, sweetheart, is a much bigger problem than who you should be dating," Donte said to her.

"Donte, don't Jesus me right now," she responded. Natasha was honestly still shaken at the irrevocable words she'd said in prayer that morning. She knew she needed to repent.

"Oh, we are just going to leave God out of what is going on with you?" he laughed at her.

Donte waited for her reaction. He knew he shouldn't laugh at her. He didn't mean anything by it, but he knew it was something that Shawn used to do to belittle her.

Natasha felt the sting of his humor nip at her insides, but she wouldn't retreat. She was a fighter now; she could take it. She would've immediately slid into a turtle shell if Shawn had done that. She looked at Donte, who had turned to face her.

"You're just…impossible sometimes," he added, choosing his words carefully. He shook his head.

"I know," she said to him.

Donte was careful not to push her into anything. He would be patient; love had pushed him to the next level of patience. There was a thought to kiss her forehead, but he decided not to. Instead, he turned and continued preparing her meal. He changed the subject to Nivea's last game they watched together to lighten the mood.

The two ate in front of the TV, with Donte insisting they watch something other than OWN. His phone rang and he stepped into the kitchen to answer it. The call lasted almost 20 minutes. Natasha gathered it was a ministry call by the reference to scriptures that she could hear from the living room. She decided that it was none of her business. Her day had begun rough, but she was happy enough in this moment. A moment of peace was just what she needed.

"Everything ok?" she couldn't help but to ask when he'd returned.

"Of course," he answered, sitting beside her again. "I'm working on something for the church. Was just following up with someone."

"Is it the Armor Bearer position for the new pastor?"

"Nah. I believe God is calling me for a greater sacrifice." He checked his watch and quickly changed the subject. "Aren't you meeting the Daughters today?"

Donte decided that while God was working to take him to the next level in his life, He'd keep silent about it until God revealed it.

"Goodness, yes," she exclaimed, jumping from the couch. "I'd almost forgotten."

In her excitement, she tripped and tumbled forward into Donte's waiting arms. He caught her abruptly, the fall forcing their bodies closer than ever. Donte tried to tell himself that the fall was an accident and that the grasp he had around her waist had nothing to do with how her perfume haunted him since they'd sat on the sofa. The way he was looking at her now had nothing to do with the way she tossed her long hair to the side when she laughed and snorted. But, the truth was, the entire moment was creating tension in regions that he knew he was too old and disciplined to succumb to. He pushed her from his lap, a little embarrassed that he hadn't let go sooner.

"I should go," he told her, trying to shake all lustful thoughts. "I'll clean up first."

Natasha hadn't actually wanted Donte to let her go. The moment was innocent, but it was also very tender. She had been avoiding him because of moments like these. She'd almost forgotten how good it felt to be touched by a man that loved her.

"You're right," Natasha decided as he picked up their dishes and walked toward the kitchen.

"We can't do anything that would mess up what God wants to do in our relationship. I can't," he said declaratively.

They both heard keys fumbling in the front door.

"Hey Ma."

In walked Nivea, Natasha's 17-year-old daughter, from basketball practice. Recently, she'd been practicing overtime since next year meant college and, hopefully, an athletic scholarship to someone's school. Every time Natasha went to a game, she saw how good her daughter was. It reminded her of her birth father, Antonio Crane, the basketball star.

"Hey baby," Natasha said, running to give her baby girl a kiss.

"I'm sweaty, Ma," Nivea said, dodging it. "I saw Donte's car out front. Is he here?"

"Hey, champ," Donte said, emerging from the kitchen. He greeted Nivea with a high five.

"I see you kept Mom company today. She needs it." Nivea said.

"Yea, but I'm leaving. I'll see you two later."

He pushed past Nivea and closed the door behind him.

"What's up with him, Mom? You still haven't answered him yet?" Nivea said, dropping her duffle bag near the door and falling into the soft couch cushions. "But judging from how hot this seat is, he's been here for a minute. I see you, Ma."

Natasha looked at her daughter incredulously and the two cracked up.

"Young lady, what I do with Donte is none of your business," said Natasha, taking a seat on the far end of the couch. "And I'll have you know that I am a woman of virtue."

She paused, moving toward her teenage daughter.

"You are too, right?" she asked.

"Mom, I'm saving myself for the man I will marry," Nivea laughed. "I don't want to go through what some of my friends are going through…baby daddies and all of that. No time for it. Just ball and school to worry about."

A wave of relief washed over Natasha and she reached to hug her daughter. It was her nightly prayer that Nivea didn't repeat the same mistakes she had.

"Yea, yea," Nivea said in the midst of their embrace. "Don't change the subject. What's up with Donte?"

The long-legged teen jumped up to see if there was food left over for her to eat. Nivea's practice uniform always made her legs look ten times longer. Today, she wore her braids back into a low bun. It was the style of a baller, she'd told Natasha; she didn't have time for press outs and sew-ins. Her life was best when she had a ball in her hands and sweat on her forehead.

"Mom, I can feel you staring at me. I hate it," called Nivea behind her. "Donte cooked? That's what's up. What are you going to tell him?"

Natasha couldn't help but stare at her beautiful daughter. With all this craziness going on around her, it was great to have her baby to keep her company.

"I don't know what I'm going to tell him yet," answered Natasha. "How do you feel about it?"

She was scared of the answer, but if she was listening to everyone else, she should at least consider her daughter's opinion as well.

"I think that he makes you happy," said Nivea, popping a bowl into the microwave and returning to sit by her mother. "You two walk around here with your inside jokes, and he likes your snorting laugh. I'd say he's a keeper. He obviously loves you."

Nivea rubbed her mother's arm for comfort.

"I know that you miss Dad," she continued, "but he's gone."

Gone, Natasha thought. Well why didn't it feel that way?

"And I know you're not looking to replace Daddy, but you need to move on. Donte wants to help you, and I think you should let him. When he's here…I don't know…it kind of feels like we have a family."

Natasha smiled and squeezed Nivea's hand. The microwave beeped and she watched her daughter run to get her food.

"Anyway, can you call Donte back over here? That scout from Penn State is coming over in like an hour. I think this is the one, Mom."

Scout visits had become a regular occurrence at the house these days. Natasha kept her abode in top shape for appearance's sake. It was usually Donte who did all the talking anyway.

"Honey, today is Deborah's Daughters, remember?" Natasha reminded her daughter. "I can cancel, though. Or tell the girls I'll be late."

"No, I think Donte can handle it. The coach will be at my next game anyway. Then you guys can meet."

"I guess that's fine," she decided, unsure of how she felt about it all. Donte only lived 10 minutes away, so he'd be able to get back within plenty of time. "Ask him and see what he says. I'll go get ready."

###

After her shower, Natasha opened her closet for the second time that day. She was glad to find a pair of favorite skinny jeans and a deep orange blazer to wear. Gaudy bangles and diamond earrings would totally set this outfit off, she thought, admiring her figure in the mirror. Running a wide-toothed comb through her long, natural hair, she tousled the sides to give it a fuller look.

Downstairs, she could hear the heard the doorbell ring for the second time which meant that the coach was here to see Nivea. She sighed with relief. At least she'd be able to meet this coach before she went to meet the girls. Shoving her cell phone in her purse, Natasha ran downstairs where she could see Donte waiting in the living room.

"Back so soon?" she asked playfully.

"I can never stay away too long," Donte responded with his own flirt.

"You guys are too much," Nivea said from her spot on the couch. They laughed in unison.

"So where is she?" Natasha asked them.

"She is a he," corrected Nivea. "And he's in the restroom. His name's Coach Tony."

"He?" asked Nivea. "Where's Coach Harris?"

"Coach Harris is on maternity leave," said a voice from around the corner. "Pleasure to see you again, Natasha. I'm Antonio Crane with the Penn State Lady Lions."

Holding his hand out for a greeting was Natasha's ex-boyfriend, the father of her first and only child.

"Um…," began Natasha, unable to breathe. "Hello."

Before she realized it, she was shaking hands with Nivea's birth father.

"Again?" asked Donte, standing beside Natasha. "You two know each other?"

"Uh…," Natasha started again. She wished she could find some air or an emergency exit at the moment. "Um, yea. Long time," was all she could muster.

"I've been through Nivea's tape a million times," said Antonio. "Your daughter is amazingly talented."

Natasha looked at her daughter, who was beaming with joy at this stranger's compliment. Little did she know, she had more in common with this man than basketball—they shared DNA. Sick at the thought, Natasha felt a violent panic attack approaching.

"I, um. I have to leave."

Natasha was truly speechless. Was this really happening? She repositioned her bag on her shoulder and turned toward the door. The cool air on the other side would be just what she needed.

"Are you ok?" Donte called after her.

"I'm fine," she responded. "Have fun, Nivea. Nice meeting… seeing you again, Antonio."

She bolted through her front door, leaving everyone staring after her.

"What on Earth was that all about?" Nivea asked.

SHENAE

Shenae was the first to arrive at their favorite coffee shop for the Deborah's Daughter meeting. The smell of coffee and warm pastries greeted her at the entrance. A few members of the staff were eager to receive her at the ladies' normal seating area, among the sea of students and other patrons tapping away at their laptops. The First Ladies had become something like celebrities as they regularly held their meetings there. The servers fought to wait on the ladies because they were great tippers and always offered an encouraging word.

Shenae sat down and ordered a round of green teas while she waited for the other ladies to arrive. She was glad that the four of them had decided to keep the group together even though she and Natasha no longer held the official title of a

First Lady. She'd been a pillar in the community, and even at the risk of losing some support from their followers, they'd kept Shenae as a member. It was Lynette, however, who had now become the face of the organization. Shenae wasn't bothered by the change; it lifted some of the pressures and questions about her personal life.

She looked out the window at the parking lot, hoping that the ladies wouldn't be late. She had agreed to meet Angelo here and didn't want the ladies questioning her about him. Pulling her compact mirror out of her purse, Shenae stole a glance at her reflection. She'd been wearing her hair natural in a twistout style and her make up was neat. She'd opted for her favorite outfit, a sleeveless purple silk blouse and a flirty skirt that brushed the top of her knees. On her feet, she wore her favorite camel colored strappy sandals. She felt beautiful, honestly, even with the heartbreak still throbbing inside of her. But she hadn't caused any heads to turn when she walked into the coffee shop, she thought. Suddenly, she held her head high and remembered that she was a woman of God. She silently chastised herself that she'd doubted who she was in that moment. After Leon's deceit, it had just been so hard to feel like she was enough anymore. In fact, each time she thought about what her husband did, she felt another moment of anger and frustration. Their story was so cliché. The pastor cheats on his devoted wife and steals money from the ministry. Cliché. That realization made her cringe.

"Keep it together," she said to herself, feeling the tears of her memories.

"Sis!" Natasha slid into the booth next to her, frantically. "I need you to pray. Pray right now. Pray that I move away and never come back."

"What?" responded a puzzled Shenae.

"I'm in trouble, Shenae," Natasha said, collapsing into her friend's arms.

Shenae held her disheveled sister and welcomed her release. She was glad she had kept it together now. That's how God is, she thought. His assignments were never on a schedule, but they were always right on time. It was now the time to let her sister lean on her. She whispered prayers in-between the quiet sobs and mouthed a quick hello to Amauri as she joined them.

"Oh, sis," Amauri said, resting her head on Natasha's upper back.

There was no time to ask any questions and certainty no time to assume. Amauri just joined her sister in silent prayers and they rocked together in intercession for whatever was troubling her.

Before long, Lynette joined them as well, wearing tired eyes that she hoped no one would notice, just as Natasha finally stopped crying. The weeping widow pulled her head up from Natasha's blouse and sat back in the booth. There was a long pause from the table as the ladies waited for Natasha to share her troubles.

"I'm sorry," Natasha apologized, looking at Shenae's tearstained blouse.

"Hopefully, this isn't because I was late," said Lynette in an attempt to lighten the mood. She reached in her purse for her stash of tissues and handed them off to Natasha. "It won't happen again. I promise."

Natasha was the first to laugh at Lynette's humor. The other ladies let out chuckles of relief in response.

"What's going on?" Amauri asked.

"Nivea's father showed up to my house today."

"Her birth father?" questioned Shenae in disbelief.

"Yes. Antonio. The school he coaches at wants her to play basketball there."

"What did Nivea say? What happened?" Lynette asked.

"Nothing. I ran out the house."

"You did what?" asked Lynette again.

"I didn't know what else to do."

"So he's just there? With Nivea? By himself?" Lynette kept the interrogation going.

"No. Donte's there too," responded Natasha. "No one knows anything. Well now they probably do. Oh no."

Natasha wiped her running mascara and began again.

"And I found out this morning that Shawn put a clause in his will that says I can't remarry for another three years," she said, pausing again to let that sink in. "And I followed that news up by kissing Donte for the first time today."

Shenae attempted to conjure up a scripture for comfort, but she couldn't. In fact, all the other sisters ran through their mental Jesus Rolodex and came up short.

"Well we're here for you," Amauri offered her sister support.

"Always."

"Anything you need."

"Thanks, ladies. Enough about me," Natasha said, handing the pack of tissues back to Lynette. "What's everyone else have going on?"

"Well, speaking of husbands," Shenae began, "Leon's sentence is being reduced. He'll be out in a few weeks."

"Wait. What?" Lynette asked, hoping she wouldn't have to share her bad news right this moment. What is God up to?, she thought. They'd learned a long time ago when Hell was breaking loose in their lives, that it was only the enemy determined to keep them from a bigger promise on the horizon. If he could distract them with the issues in their lives, then they would never move forward into their respective promises.

"A few weeks. And he wants us to reconcile," Shenae said. "Oh, and I think the guy that's coming over here is my blind date."

The ladies looked up to see a tall, buff glass of gorgeous walking toward them. Shenae spotted him coming in the café during Natasha's confession. He had taken a seat at the bar and blatantly stared at her since. He was taller than she imagined, taller than Leon. She cursed herself with the comparison to her ex, but it was all she had to go by. His skin looked nearly edible, a tanned caramel. His jet-black hair was curly and longer than she thought a man should wear it, but it looked good on him. Shenae set her eyes on his broad, strong shoulders next. They made him stand up incredibly straight. In response, she felt herself suck her stomach in and correct her horrible posture. She was straining to find anything imperfect about this gorgeous stranger.

"Excuse me, ladies," said the gentleman, exposing a set of too white teeth. Shenae noticed that his slightly crooked smile was possibly his only flaw. But that didn't matter because the dimple in his left cheek put the nail in the coffin of all her over stimulated senses.

"You wouldn't happen to be Shenae, would you?" he asked, looking at her.

She just sat looking up at him in response. Amauri jabbed her in the side to signal her to get up and address their new guest.

"I am," she held her hand out to him. "Angelo?"

"Yes, ma'am," he said shaking her hand. "Is this your Deborah's

Daughters meeting?"

She looked at the other women around the table. Each was gawking at him, sure to make him uncomfortable soon. Shenae was equally as uncomfortable. Her blouse was wrinkled now with eye makeup stains on the sleeve.

"Uh, yea. It is. This is Amauri, Lynette, and Natasha," said Shenae, introducing him to the group.

"Nice to meet you all," he said, smiling again and exposing his insanely pearly whites. "I don't want to interrupt. Just wanted to introduce myself. I'll be waiting at the bar."

Angelo turned and left Shenae in awe of how he looked from the back. Shenae knew that she had just turned a bright shade of ruby through her mocha skin. She felt like a giddy schoolgirl; she hadn't felt anything from a man in such a long time. She would have to sit down and process what just happened to her.

"So listen," Amauri jarred her from her thoughts. "If things don't work out with me and BP, I'd be glad to take him off your hands."

The four of them fell back in their places in the booth and laughed, the heartiness of the moment refreshing their meeting. As Lynette called the meeting to order, Shenae stole a glance toward the bar at Angelo who was looking in her direction. He lifted his coffee towards her. She couldn't help but get excited at the notion that he was watching her.

"So let's begin with a word of prayer," said Lynette. "It seems like we all need it."

Father in the name of Jesus, we just want to tell you 'thank you.' We are so blessed that in the midst of a storm, God, you are still in control...

The ladies went on for the next hour as if none of them had any turmoil in their respective lives. They finalized plans for Amauri and Bishop Paden's going away party at the end of the month. Shenae, Lynette, and Natasha began to plan a trip to New York to see them. Shenae even tossed around the idea of having Amauri start a new Deborah's Daughter chapter in her home state.

"Ok, ladies," said Shenae, eyeing Angelo again. "I think that's all, right?"

She had been unable to focus the entire meeting. The heat flowing in her direction from Angelo was enough to keep her occupied in her own thoughts. *Lawd Jesus, he is fine*, she heard herself mumble under her breath once while Lynette was talking.

"Are we keeping you from something?" asked Amauri, noticing Shenae was obviously smitten. "I can order you a cold shower, sis."

They all laughed as Shenae turned a deeper shade of red in embarrassment. None of them had seen her so affected like this by a man. She didn't even seem to budge emotionally when her marriage failed. She took it hard, of course, but she never showed them one sign of her anguish.

The ladies agreed it was time to let Shenae have her fun and they gave each other hugs goodbye. None of the ladies had an answer for their respective life stresses, but there were words of encouragement exchanged and friendship and laughter to take home with them that evening.

Angelo, seeing the group dissipate, came over.

"Ladies, I hope to see you all very soon," he said, flashing those gorgeous white teeth again.

"Same here," they all seemed to say in unison.

"Goodbye, ladies," Shenae said, her eyes urging them to leave the café so her date could officially begin.

The ladies walked out, leaving a very nervous Shenae standing in front of Angelo at the booth.

"So where should we sit?" Shenae asked.

"Why don't we go outside on the patio?" he offered. "It's a little warm in here."

They walked together and reached the door, where Angelo pushed it open before she had a chance to consider opening it. He then pulled out the chair at the table they decided upon and allowed her to sit down. Shenae had to admit that she was pleasantly surprised by his efforts at chivalry; for a man 13 years younger than her, he sure had manners. She couldn't remember the last time Leon had taken the time out to open a door for her. It was such a small thing, but it made her smile.

Sitting down, a waft of air drifted his cologne in her direction. She silenced the attraction that made her want to reach out and touch him. The feel of his strength was sure to calm the storms that life were threatening to shake her to pieces. That was the smell of a real man, but she had been fooled before. She couldn't be that same girl who fell in love with the man from the flower shop; that girl had been foolish and had fallen love with a lie.

Shenae ordered a second green tea and Angelo ordered another coffee. As the server left, they both looked at the other and started talking at the same time.

"I'm sorry. Go ahead" Angelo apologized.

"So, let's get this out of the way," Shenae began. "This is clearly a bad idea. We can have this one date and then I think we should just call this whole thing off. It's silly. I don't know what I was thinking."

The words shocked Shenae just as much as they did Angelo. She knew that she must have been crazy to object to spending time with anyone that she was this magnetically drawn to, but heartbreak was inevitable. He was young; she wasn't. He seemed open to dating; she had barely gotten her bearings in the divorcee world. In fact, she convinced herself, she was doing him a favor by telling him this was going nowhere.

"I was thinking that your profile picture didn't do you justice,"

Angelo responded, clearly ignoring her last words.

"Wait. Did you hear what I just said?" the flattered Shenae tried to change the subject.

"You're beautiful," he added. "And afraid."

"Afraid? Look, if this is your attempt at getting me to change my mind, you failed," Shenae began to rise from the table. "This is just not going to work out."

She started to walk toward the door to the café. Angelo quickly rose and grabbed her arm. He pulled her into him and wrapped his arms around her. Shenae didn't fight the embrace. She'd never felt anything like what she was feeling from a man before, but she couldn't pull away. It took a second for her to realize that he was whispering a prayer into her ear. He was praying for her. She caught herself almost letting her wall down, and suddenly, he released her.

"I am not here to cause you pain," he said to her. "I'm here to help you see that on the other side of that pain is beauty."

She looked back at him, unable to speak or move.

"Let's just be friends," he offered. "And if God says otherwise, then we'll go from there. Right now, I'd love for you to sit again so that I can get to know you a little better."

Angelo held his hand out for her to take the open chair she'd just abandoned.

"What do you think?" he asked her.

How could she say no to that? She had looked into his deep brown eyes and, ultimately, heard from God. She hadn't told him anything about Leon, but Angelo's words seemed to speak directly to the wounds her ex-husband had caused. She'd been punishing herself for so long because of him. She had just met Angelo, and after that prayer, Shenae felt like she'd been reunited with an old friend.

"I think that is a great idea," she said, taking the seat. "Thanks, Angelo."

Angelo took the seat across from her again and smiled.

"While I still have your attention," he said, his pearly whites beaming, "I need you to know that none of what you're going through is your fault. His mistakes, his judgments...whoever he is...they aren't your fault."

It was as if he had read her mind. And just like that, the two were talking like they'd been friends forever.

LYNETTE

It had been almost a week since Lynette had heard her husband reveal to her that he may have fathered another son with another woman. Since then, they'd also learned that Harriet's son was sick with a possibly terminal illness and would need a blood transfusion. That was what originally led them to discover Harriet's husband was not his father.

Since then, Lynette had spent hours meditating in her prayer closet. She had practically paced a hole in the floor.

Father God, grant me serenity to accept the things I cannot change…and to fully trust You in the meantime. In Jesus' name, Amen.

Lynette finished her prayer and exited her holy haven to fine her husband reading a book in their bed. She walked toward him to place her Bible in the nightstand.

"Sweetheart, how did everything turn out from the last Deborah's Daughters meeting?" Pastor Andre asked her. "It was almost a week ago, but I haven't heard a peep from you about it."

"Oh, it was crazy," Lynette responded. She had to admit it was the most exhausting meeting the ladies had in a while. "All four of us seem to have a lot going on right now. I managed to keep myself together though."

"Did you tell them about what happened?" her husband asked.

"I didn't, actually," she admitted.

It was true that Lynette had become more open with her husband in the past months, but she was still working on letting others in. She had thought about sharing the news with Amauri when she saw her at church on Sunday but decided otherwise. She just wanted this one between her and God for now.

"Oh," said a confused Pastor Andre. "I know we having talked about it much. I've been busy with Bishop Paden's move and the added pastoral training. Do you want to talk about it, babe?"

"Have you heard anything else?" she asked without hesitation. She wouldn't shy away from the subject with her husband. She was waiting for him to take a test that could potentially change their lives.

"No. I'm still scheduled to go and take the test tomorrow. We should get the results soon after."

Lynette ran her fingers through her hair at his response. Andre put his book down and reached for her hand.

"No matter what, you're still with me, right?" he asked, motioning for her to come closer.

Lynette noticed immediately that his voice was uncertain. Here he was, having to relive his personal failure in front of her once again. They had both been guilty of letting their minds wander to a hypothetical future if the child turned out to be Andre's. Every visit would be a reminder that he'd betrayed their love and trust. And Lynette could sense that no matter how much validation she gave her husband, he would never truly be over his own personal disappointment.

"Andre, I can't say that what happened doesn't still haunt me sometimes," she said, sitting beside him on the bed. "The reality is that you slept with another woman. It's something we have to face, but understand that we will face it together. I made a vow when we pulled through that storm to never leave you uncovered again…to stay in the ring with you."

She cupped his face in her hands and continued.

"I am praying for you not just as my husband but as my friend," she said, kissing him.

She pulled back to see him smiling again.

"It's important to note that, whatever the outcome, you will owe me major diamonds," she finished, gesturing toward her delicate fingers for effect. "Major!"

Andre laughed and pulled her into his arms. He gladly gave into the sensual draw of her kiss and the movement of her body against his.

The blinking nuisance on their nightstand interrupted their moment.

"Babe, you're ringing," Pastor Andre said.

"Oh, I'm about to ring alright."

"No," Andre said, breaking their lip lock. "Really, sweetheart, your phone is ringing."

"Oh," she laughed, reaching for her cell.

It was an unknown number, which was typical for ministry calls. She grabbed the phone to answer it in another room. She motioned toward the bedside clock to alert Andre that it was almost time for him to leave for his meeting that night with Bishop Paden.

She stepped into the hallway and made her way toward their home office. Sliding her thumb up on the phone's face to answer, she said hello three times.

"Um, hello?" she decided a fourth before hanging up.

"Hello, Lynn...um, First Lady," came a woman's voice finally.

There was silence on Lynette's part now. The sound of the woman's voice, even after so much time, still produced a shiver inside of her. It was a moment she swore she'd been waiting for, but it turned out, she wasn't ready at all for this.

"First Lady, it's Harriet."

Lynette knew who it was. Still, she remained silent. For months, she'd imagined so many times exactly what she'd say to this woman who tore her life apart.

"How did you get my number?" Lynette found herself asking. She could hear the garage door in her house going up, which meant her husband was leaving for his meeting. And here she was chatting with his former mistress.

"Someone at the church gave it to me," Harriet responded.

Lynette noted that Harriet sounded timid over the phone.

"I need to talk to you. Are you available to talk?" Harriet pleaded. "Could I meet you somewhere?"

Seeing her was absolutely out of the question, Lynette thought. She could feel deep-seated rage bubbling in her torso at the audacity of this woman. What was there to talk about? Would they share Andre sex stories over a late-night latte?

"Listen, Harriet," Lynette said as calmly as possible, "The outcome of the paternity test will be between you and my husband. We have nothing to discuss."

Lynette wasn't even planning on going with Andre when he went in for the test. She knew that if Harriet was there, she couldn't be held responsible for what might transpire.

"And as a matter of fact, I don't think it would be in your best interest to be in the same room with me," Lynette added.

People often mistook the demure and position of a First Lady as something they were born with. Lynette only needed a good enough reason to remind Harriet that she was a totally different woman before the title. But now, she didn't have to be disrespectful to Harriet. The woman had done a good enough job on her own to disrespect herself.

Lynette took a breath and was about to say something else but heard sobs on the other end of the line.

"I am so sorry, First Lady," Harriet cried. "I never meant to hurt you, you know? Or fall for Pastor Andre. I was stupid to let him confiding in me mean something different. He loves you so much."

Hearing Harriet apologize and confirm her husband's love for her in the same breath was not what Lynette was expecting. She was listening to Harriet cry uncontrollably now.

"You two have two beautiful children," she began again. "I can't imagine what I am going to do if I lose my son. It feels like God is punishing me."

That was enough to shake down anyone's defenses. And with Harriet's sobs flooding Lynette's ear, the First Lady could only feel sorry for her. Sure, she'd done wrong, but if there was one thing that Lynette had learned through all this, it was that forgiveness was not about the person who wronged you. The benefit, however, was that forgiveness freed the transgressor. Harriet had been standing still all this time, needing Lynette to forgive her. She was holding on to all the pain as if it had happened yesterday. Lynette knew it was wrong to continue to harbor ill will toward her.

"Harriet, look. I can't say that I will ever understand what happened between you and my husband," Lynette began once Harriet took a breath from crying. "But I want you to know that what is happening right now is not punishment for what you did. If you asked God for forgiveness, then that's what you received."

Lynette looked up and thanked God for the words he was imparting into her at that moment. She was glad she had been in her prayer closet this week; she knew she wouldn't be able to do this without Him.

"The only one still holding this is you," Lynette continued. "Your son being sick is awful, but the Word says, 'All things work together for the good.' God is working a greater good in it for you…even in sickness…even in death."

It wasn't what she thought she'd ever say to Harriet, but it was the right thing to say. Lynette's heart was full knowing that God was shining through that conversation.

"Thank you so much, First Lady. I appreciate that." Harriet said, sniffling on the other end.

For the next few minutes, Lynette was a listening ear as Harriet described what she and her husband had been going through with her son's illness. All the while, she kept thinking that God always seemed to amaze her. Two years ago, she'd wanted to physically damage this woman, and now, she was offering her solace in her time of need.

"Harriet, I'm actually home right now and need to prepare dinner for my family," said Lynette, attempting to end the conversation. She could hear Ivory crying from her crib, which meant that Benny would also be waking up from his nap. "I'll be praying for your son. Have a good night."

She and Harriet exchanged goodbyes and Lynette disconnected the call. She hung up the phone feeling ever grateful for her wonderful family and the blessings God had given them. Walking into her children's room, Lynette picked up her daughter and put on a DVD for her son to watch. She realized it'd been about a week since she'd been intimate with her husband. She walked downstairs to the kitchen thinking that, tonight, she'd show him just how special he was to her.

She set Ivory down in her walker and gave her a fresh bottle. Looking at the clock, she figured it would be about an hour and a half before Andre would be back. Lynette started preparing her husband's favorite meal—grilled pork chops with Marsala sauce, collard greens and wild rice. She then fixed a quick dinner for the kids and called in a favor to their in-home nanny.

"Hey Francine," began Lynette over the phone. "Would you mind taking the babies for the evening in your suite? I will make sure that it is added to your salary for the week."

Francine lived out back in their in-law suite they'd built after Ivory was born. She rarely refused a favor, so Lynette had already packed an overnight bag for her children.

"Of course, Ms. Lynette," responded Francine. "You hadn't asked me in a while. I was hoping everything was ok."

Lynette thanked God for sending them such a treasure in a nanny. She was always available to help, and she loved their children as if they were her own.

"Great. I'll have them packed up and ready to go after they eat. Thanks, Francine."

She hung up the phone and called Benny downstairs.

"Guess who's coming to get you for a sleepover tonight?...Francine!"

Benny and Ivory squealed in delight. As they ate their dinner, Lynette felt like Supermom. And tonight, she would be Superwife.

The jets of her hot tub relaxed Lynette completely as she laid her head back against the cool tile wall. It had been a crazy evening, but God proved that He always had his hand over her life. Minutes later, she found herself standing naked in front of her mirror, admiring the new curves her last pregnancy had given her. As a model, Lynette had always been incredibly thin—and she still was—but now, there was just a little something extra for her husband to grab onto when they made love.

Hearing the doorbell ring, Lynette threw on her silk robe and made her way downstairs. She wasn't expecting anyone at this hour, and Andre was due home in the next 10 minutes.

She cracked the door and peeked her head out. It was her mechanic.

"Hey there," she greeted him. "Can I help you?"

"Hello ma'am," he responded. "I was just bringing back the Jaguar from the shop," he said, pointing to her husband's second toy in the driveway. Figured I'd save you guys the trip."

"Oh, that's right," she remembered, opening the door fully. "My husband left me money to pay you. Come inside. He'll be here any minute."

Lynette let the man in and went to retrieve her purse from the bottom of the stairs. She bent down, unaware that she was being watched.

"Mighty nice view from where I'm standing, ma'am," she heard his voice behind her say.

"Sir," she said, turning around startled. "My husband should be pulling in any minute now. I'm sure he'd be less than pleased to find you staring at his wife with that look."

Lynette clutched the robe closer to her body and tried to remain calm.

"How about I take a different type of payment," the man in her foyer said, undressing her with his eyes.

"Sir, this is very inappropriate," Lynette said, listening for the garage door to open. "Please leave before I call someone."

She was trying to be brave but she knew that soon she would be lost in her overwhelming fear.

"You're not calling anyone," the man said, coming toward her and grabbing her arm. He pressed her hard against the wall, and Lynette could feel the rigid length of him rising through the pants he wore.

"Please don't hurt me," Lynette pleaded with him.

The warm feeling of fear crept up her spine as she prepared herself for what was coming next. His lips crushed hers. She tried to fight him, but he forced her mouth open. His tongue darted inside her mouth as she thrashed and bucked from the wall. His hands unfolded her robe and it dropped to the floor. His eyes traveled up and down her body, taking in the fullness of her breasts and thighs. She should have been appalled by his gross satisfaction of her body.

"God, you are beautiful," he said, and she softened.

She loved it when Pastor Andre played her mechanic, but she especially loved it when he slipped from character and became her doting husband. He pushed her again into the wall, causing her to wrap her long legs around him. Her flesh awakened as the heat from Pastor Andre's trousers met with her moist skin. With each kiss, they fought each other. Lynette was greedy for more of the taste of her husband, and he was equally as greedy.

She moaned in his mouth, causing him to completely slip out of character. He undid his pants and dropped them to the ground, wanting his naked flesh to join hers. As they rode the wall in passion, the friction he applied to her was stirring the pressure in her belly. It didn't matter that he hadn't entered her yet. She was getting off from the rough jolts against the wall and his breaths in her ear. Frantically searching for her release, she rode him harder. As she felt her climax coming, she tore from his kiss and yelled in ecstasy, trembling beneath him. Beads of sweat rolled down her breast as she tried to steady her body from what they'd just shared. She laughed into his neck as Andre carried her up the stairs to their bedroom.

He tenderly laid her onto the bed, letting her rest a minute.

"That was fun," he said, commenting on their rendezvous downstairs.

"I made you dinner," she said. "Your favorite."

"I think I'll have dessert first."

He climbed on top of her and pulled at her nipples with his teeth. They stood erect and ready for him. Andre was always ready to please his wife; as an amazing mother and life partner, she deserved it all.

Lynette slid back on the bed to allow him to service her from the edge.

"Don't worry," he told her, sensing what she wanted. "I've got you."

Pastor Andre's face was filled with as much fire as she had coursing through her. Lynette didn't worry anymore. She trusted him; she trusted that not only did he have her in this moment, but he would have her for the rest of their lives.

Raising his head to find her eyes, he looked at her. She was biting her lip in anticipation for the affection to come. She'd never gotten used to the way he just stared at her when they were making love. It made her shy, like it was their first time. She watched as her husband grabbed her thighs and pulled her legs up and open. She was completely vulnerable to his masterful fingers. He ran his fingers up and down her dewy skin, then firmly grabbed her ankles to bend her knees and place her feet on the bed.

He looked at her sweet treasure calling his name. Lynette closed her eyes as he bent to honor her with his kisses. Andre was gentle at first as he licked and filled her with his tongue. The sounds of his lapping were enough to drive her over the edge, but each time he sensed her climax, he'd pull back.

"Not tonight," he warned, coming up for air. "You let me take my time."

There was no point in objecting that command from his sexy voice. She tilted her head back in delight as he drank her in for as long as she could take him. She squirmed and lifted her body from the bed as he drove her crazy with pleasure. Now, he'd have to wrap his hands around her thighs to keep her still. She was soaking him as her juices ran down the sides of his mouth.

"Babe, I need you now," she moaned, pulling away from him.

Hearing her plea, Pastor Andre rose up and lifted his shirt over his head. This time, it was her turn to admire him. He was so sexy, she thought to herself. Andre was no ordinary Baptist preacher. His muscles were rigid and sexy. His skin glistened from the heat that they had been sharing. He was gorgeous, and the best part was that he was all hers. He walked to turn on their stereo. Andre loved the soundtrack of Jazz greats as he made love to his wife.

Coming back to her, he broke through her wetness and gave her just the tip of him. Sliding in and out with the head of his steel member, she cried out in ecstasy.

"I want all of you," she told him when she couldn't take any more.

Her plea was so sexy to him. Lynette grabbed her husband and pushed him onto his back. Making her way onto him, she felt weightless and on top of the world.

"I love you, babe…so much," he told her as she put him inside of her, her hips and his fully connecting.

She smiled at his declaration and moved her hips ferociously in response, back and forth and up and down. His grunts were a sign that she was driving him crazy. She rode him at a harder pace, her hands grabbing his chest. Lynette could see him trying to keep it together, which only made her want to drive him crazier. When his hands grabbed her hips firmly and stilled her, she knew she'd done her job.

"That was yummy, Pastor" Lynette said, jumping off of him and throwing on his T-shirt.

Pastor Andre just lay there, staring at the ceiling in ecstasy, while his hyper wife sashayed back to the bed. Even in the moonlight, he could see the curve of her perfect bottom dance for his eyes only.

"I'll take that dinner now," he told her, sitting up. "And an ice cold glass of water."

Lynette kissed him and pulled him off the bed so they could return downstairs.

"And then," she added. "Another round of dessert."

NATASHA

Nivea, I don't really know how to say this, but...Antonio is your father.

Niv, baby...This is the hardest thing for me to say. You know Mommy doesn't normally keep anything from you, but...I wanted to protect you.

Oh, Nivea. Please try to understand that I thought I was doing what was best for you.

For almost two weeks now, Natasha had been struggling with how to tell Nivea that her father had made an appearance in her life.

When the shock of him popping up had worn off, Natasha reached out to Antonio to question his motives. She and Antonio shared a conversation in which he stated that he'd be staying in town for a little while longer. They had agreed that Nivea deserved to know the truth, but Antonio was pressing Natasha to tell Nivea before he left in the next few days for another scouting trip.

Natasha hadn't spilled her secret to Donte either. He was growing suspicious at the way this coach had taken so much interest in Natasha. Coming to a few games was one thing, but sitting in on every practice and offering to drive Nivea to and from school was another. He'd even been to church with them twice now. Donte had begun asking questions that Natasha wasn't ready to answer, which only made the sometimes awkwardness between them even worse.

But Nivea was seemingly unsuspicious. In fact, Natasha had never seen her daughter so happy. In this entanglement of secrets, Nivea's smile had become the silver lining. Natasha would hate to see it go away.

"Niv, I'm home," Natasha called as she entered the living room of their condo.

She was greeted by a very excited Nivea, eager to tell her the good news.

"Mom. Coach Tony said he knows for sure that I'll have a spot on next year's team at Penn State. Isn't that great?"

Natasha kissed her 17-year-old daughter on the forehead.

"That's great sweetheart. I'm so happy for you," she said, taking a seat on the couch to sift through the mail.

Antonio had already shared the news with Natasha a few days before. He wanted Nivea to stay with him in Pennsylvania. He wanted to buy her a car to commute to school. He had shared so much, wanting to make up for all the years he'd missed in his daughter's life.

"Mom, what's wrong?" asked Nivea, sensing something was off. "Is it because the school is so far away? I'll come visit every break if we're not playing or practicing. I promise."

"Baby, no. It's not that," Natasha responded. "I'm fine, just tired. I really am happy for you."

"Well Coach Tony said he wants to take the two of us out to celebrate. I told him 6 p.m. was good. I figured we could all go to our favorite Mexican restaurant."

Antonio wanted to use this dinner as a chance to also tell Nivea the truth. Natasha had been OK with it at first, but now she wasn't so sure.

"Um…," Natasha hesitated. She wanted to just call the whole thing off and go hide under her covers.

"Come on, Mom," her daughter said. "It's one dinner. Plus I want to hear how you and Coach Tony know each other. He said you two go way back."

Oh, if only you knew, Natasha thought to herself at that moment. How could she tell her daughter that Antonio had given up his opportunity to father her when he chose another woman over the life that he had promised Natasha? She just wasn't ready to revisit that.

Natasha's phone rang in her purse on the coffee table. It was Donte.

"Hey Donte," answered Natasha.

"Hey stranger, how are you?" he asked. "I haven't heard from you in a few days. I just wanted to make sure you and Nivea are doing alright."

"Oh, we're fine, just about to go out to dinner to celebrate."

"Yea. Nivea told me Penn State it is!"

Natasha could hear Donte beaming with pride through the phone.

"Have you talked to Coach Tony?" he asked.

"Um, he's actually the one taking us out to celebrate," she responded a little hesitantly.

"Oh."

There was a silent moment shared as Donte again tried to figure out just how close this coach was getting to Natasha.

"Hey," Natasha said, interrupting his thoughts. "Come with us, please? You're just as much a part of the celebration as I am."

Plus, Natasha noted silently, she needed all the support she could get if Antonio was going to force her to drop the bomb that evening.

"Absolutely. Anything for Niv," Donte breathed a sigh of relief. "Actually, you know what? I'll pick you guys up."

"That's ok," said Natasha, about to make things awkward again. "Anton—Coach Tony is supposed to be coming to get us. Just meet us at Don Tello's at 6."

Antonio's SUV pulled into Natasha's driveway at 5:30. Answering the door, Natasha noticed that he'd traded his usual athletic apparel for a suit jacket and khakis.

"You look nice," she stepped outside to greet him.

"Thanks," he said, checking her out. "So do you."

Natasha turned to call back into the house.

"Nivea, let's go. Lock the door behind you."

They walked to his SUV together in silence, neither sure who would break the ice first.

"I invited Donte. I hope that's ok," Natasha said.

"I don't think it's best he be there when we tell her," responded Antonio. "But ok."

Just great, thought Natasha, he hadn't forgotten. They'd still be addressing the biggest secret of her life over dinner.

"So what's up with the two of you anyway?" asked Antonio.

He was aware that Natasha's husband had passed a while ago and was curious as to how close she was with this new man in her life.

"Donte?" Natasha was a little taken aback. That was a forward question and not one she felt comfortable answering. "Oh, it's… well, it's complicated."

They reached Antonio's Tahoe and he came around to open the passenger's side door. Natasha could see Nivea coming out of the house. She had changed into a nice sundress with sandals and pulled her braids pulled into a high bun.

"Hey, Coach Tony!" she called, joining them by the car in a flash.

"You look very pretty, Niv," Natasha complimented her daughter as she took her seat in the Tahoe.

"Oh, Ma, it's just a dress," Nivea said, kidding. "Thanks."

Antonio helped her into the SUV and got behind the wheel.

"You'll have to fight the boys off of you at Penn State," said Antonio, starting the car. "Or I will."

Natasha cringed, hoping Nivea didn't hear the second part of his statement.

As they rode to Don Tello's together, Nivea filled the car of stories from her past two seasons of basketball. She talked of how she didn't know she had talent until two years ago when she tried out on a whim and ended up not only on the Varsity team but also as a starter. Antonio shot a "she gets it from her Daddy" look at Natasha. In return, Natasha avoided his eyes and stared out the window in silence.

All of a sudden, a familiar song came on the radio.

I can't sleep at night | I toss and turn | Listenin' for the telephone

It was Bobby Brown's "Every Little Step," one of Antonio and Natasha's favorite songs from decades ago.

"But when I get your call, I'm all choked up. Can't believe you called my home," Antonio sang in Natasha's direction. "Come on, T-Shae, help me out."

He grabbed her leg playfully to convince her to take the next part of the song. At the next red light, he began mimicking the dance moves from the music video. A smile broke on Natasha's face at his silliness.

"Come on, T-Shae. Take the chorus," said Antonio, singing again. "...It's like that, it's like that."

Soon, she found herself joining in and belting through the next verse. It was as if the two had completely forgotten that anyone else was in the car. They'd gone nearly 18 years without speaking, but the chemistry between them was evident. Their complicated history was erased at that moment, with Antonio adding extra ad-libs to the song and Natasha unable to contain her laughter at times.

"Ha!," Natasha hollered. "You were always such a fool."

"If I remember correctly, so were y—," Antonio started.

"Umm, what just happened?" Nivea chimed in, cutting him off. "And who is T-Shae?"

Natasha immediately stopped laughing and snapped around to see a puzzled Nivea in the back seat. Oh, Bobby Brown, you've gotten me into trouble once again, she thought.

"That, um," said Natasha, trying to explain. She grabbed her daughter's hand.

"That used to be me and your mom's song," Antonio snatched the reigns of the conversation.

"What?" Nivea asked, even more puzzled.

"She deserves to know," he shrugged at Natasha when she snapped her head again to look at him. "And T-Shae was my nickname for her."

His declarations hung in the silent air. Natasha didn't know how Nivea would respond.

"Your song?" Natasha heard her daughter ask. "Like, you were together? Oh my God, Mom, you dated a ball player? Why didn't you tell me?"

"Yes, honey. Before you, Mommy had a life," she said, thankful that they had arrived at the restaurant so she could temporarily avert the range of questions Nivea had just thrown her way.

"Oh, look, there's Donte," Natasha commented as they pulled into a parking spot.

She quickly exited the vehicle and almost ran to him.

"Thanks so much for coming," Natasha said, hugging him.

He hugged her back, taking in her scent and smiling. He hadn't realized how much he had missed her until now. They waited together while Antonio and Nivea caught up with them. Now that he was looking at them together, side-by-side, Donte noticed that the two could pass for relatives. The wheels in his head couldn't fully begin to turn as Natasha suddenly locked her arm in his and they entered the restaurant. With all that was brewing in the atmosphere, Natasha knew she'd need him soon.

"How many?" the hostess asked them when they'd entered.

"Four, please," answered Donte and Antonio simultaneously.

"Ok. There's a five-to-ten minute wait. What's the name?" she asked.

"Smith."

"Crane."

Both men had answered at the same time again. The hostess shot a confused look in their direction.

"Crane," Antonio said again.

"Crane, no problem."

Antonio shot the hostess a satisfied look and went to sit by Nivea on one of the benches. Natasha looked at Donte and could see that he was a little annoyed.

"Where have you been the last few days?" Donte asked her suddenly. "Is there something wrong with your phone?"

"I'm sorry, Donte," she said, hoping he wasn't too upset with her for being out of touch lately.

"And this coach," he continued, motioning in Antonio's direction. "I did some research. You two went to the same college?"

Natasha's expression of horror confirmed his question.

"Crane, party of four!"

Saved by the hostess, Natasha thought. They all followed her to the table together and sat down. Sitting across from Nivea at the standalone table with both men at her sides, Natasha studied Donte's expression.

Since they'd taken their seats, he hadn't taken his eyes off Antonio. Weeks ago, it seemed as if the two men would be friends. But now it was obvious that the atmosphere had changed.

After the waitress had come over and taken their drink orders, there was an eerie silence at the table. Nivea and Antonio both broke that silence by leaning their heads to the left to crack their necks. Donte's senses perked up. It was the last link to the puzzle he'd been putting together in his head. He shot a glance at Natasha whose face held that same horrified look as before.

"Donte, did you know my mom and Coach Tony used to date?" Nivea asked at what Natasha felt couldn't have been a worse time. "She used to date a ball player. How cool is that?"

Natasha could hear her heartbeat drowning out the sound of her thoughts as she waited for Donte to answer. He didn't.

"Here's your Diet Coke," the waitress said, beginning to hand out the drinks.

"Yea, so how long ago was that that you two used to date?" Donte asked once they'd put in their food orders.

"About 18 years ago," Antonio spoke up before Natasha could say anything.

No, Natasha thought, this was not the way that this was going to happen. She had to take control of this before things got worse.

"18 years? So before my mom met my dad, huh?" Nivea paused, not noticing that Natasha was mortified at how close she was to knowing the truth. "Um…did you know him?"

Natasha found herself tearing up at the table. She quickly tried to wipe her tears away.

"Oh my God, Mom. I'm sorry," apologized Nivea. "I was just curious."

"No, baby. I'm the one who's sorry," said Natasha, beginning to cry. She looked at Antonio and then back at Nivea. "I'm so sorry."

Sensing that his assumption was dead on, Donte grabbed Natasha's hand to comfort her.

"What is going on?" Nivea asked, looking around the table.

Antonio was silent. Telling Nivea seemed so much easier when he tried it in his head. But now he realized how complicated this would all become after she knew. She would have questions; he wouldn't have answers. He might break her heart with all his past acts of cowardice; she might break his by never speaking to him again. He looked at Natasha, the strong, beautiful woman he'd abandoned for the thrill of the perks that came with being a young athlete back then. Women were throwing themselves at him, and he was with it at first until he realized how empty he was without Natasha. In fact, he'd almost gone back to her when he realized the error of his ways. But he found out that she had birthed a child that was undoubtedly his, and the thought of being a father shook him to his core. But it shifted his motivation. He swore when he made it to the league, he'd come back for his family. But the injury during his first off-season ruined all his plans...

"Mom, why are you crying?"

Gathering herself, Natasha attempted to grab ahold of her peace and say a quick prayer.

"Let's grab hands, everyone," Natasha said.

It was the only thing she could think of that would stop the tornado brewing in front of her.

"No, Mom. I will not join hands. Don't try to cover up this up with a God moment. What is going on?"

Natasha wanted to chasten her daughter for her tone, but the truth was that she did owe her an explanation.

"Mom," Nivea began again, her eyes filled with tears. "I'm going to ask you a question, and I need you to answer me."

"Baby, calm down. I just don't think that this is the appropriate time," Natasha said, getting up to go over to her.

Donte and Antonio stood up in response, neither sure of what to do. Natasha moved to rub her daughter's shoulder and calm her but Nivea pulled back. The look she shot her mother as she stood up almost shattered Natasha's heart to pieces. She had never seen her daughter like this. Even during her teenage rants, she had never pulled away from her.

Nivea turned and ran into Donte's arms, crying.

"Did you know too, Donte?" Nivea asked him.

"I just figured it out, champ," he told her. "Come on. Sit down. Let's hear your mom out, ok?"

Natasha wanted to crawl into a hole seeing her daughter deny her and then accept Donte's comfort. It was breaking her heart to watch her daughter crying and know that she was the reason for those tears. When she'd told Nivea that her father had been killed in a car accident while she was pregnant, it was to keep her safe. She never thought that she'd be a single parent again. And she certainly hadn't imagined that Antonio would come back in her life.

They all sat down again at the table. Nivea laid her head on Donte's shoulder and waited for her mother to respond.

"Nivea, I need you to know that Mommy wanted to tell you so many times, but I just couldn't," Natasha began to explain.

For the next few minutes, Natasha tried to detail the circumstances surrounding her pregnancy in college. Antonio chimed in when he could but mostly remained quiet, afraid that Nivea's anger would get the best of her again.

"...And then I met Shawn at church and he promised to always provide for us, promised that we'd never want for anything. So I married him and left the past in the past," finished Natasha. "I'm so sorry. I promise I didn't do any of this to hurt you."

"You lied to me, Ma," cried Nivea, still in Donte's arms. "You let me think that God left me fatherless...just so you wouldn't have to deal with your own issues."

Natasha put her hands in her face and fell into pieces.

"Nivea!" she heard Donte and Antonio call.

She looked up to see her daughter dash from the table and run out of the restaurant, something she thought only happened in movies.

"That was so hard," Natasha sighed, grabbing her napkin to wipe her tearstained face. "I never thought I'd ever make her cry like that."

It was hard for Donte to watch the scene unfold as well, but knew that it needed to happen. He only wished Natasha had told him instead of letting him figure it out himself. If she had come to him, maybe he could've done something to help. Donte wanted to go outside to comfort Nivea, but the woman he loved was crumbling before him. He saw Antonio about to comfort Natasha and found himself filled with anger.

"I think you should go and check on your daughter," Donte said firmly. "That is why you've come back into her life, right? To be there for her?"

His words dripped with more venom than he wanted, but Donte wanted to make sure that Antonio understood that his arrival in their life was for Nivea and not for Natasha.

"You're right. Excuse me," Antonio said.

He got up from the table and walked toward the door. Donte saw him find the waitress and give her his credit card for their dinners before he went outside to find Nivea.

"Natasha, sweetie," Donte moved closer to Natasha and she fell into his arms. He embraced her and they sat there for a while. The waitress came and brought all their food in to-go boxes. Once Natasha felt the disappointment wash away, she lifted her head.

"I must look a mess," she told him. "I'm so tired of crying, Donte."

"You still look beautiful to me," Donte said, brushing a wayward strand of hair away from her eyes.

He was angry with her, but he still loved her. He was looking at her now the way every woman wanted to be looked at after a wrenching heartbreak.

"This too shall pass," Donte encouraged her with a kiss on the forehead. As he grabbed the side of her face, it only seemed right for his lips to find hers. The kiss was short and sweet. Almost as soon as their lips touched, he pulled way.

"Antonio found us again after Shawn died," Natasha explained. "I'd done such a splendid job of falling off the radar that he lost us for years, but he never gave up on finding us."

Pastor Shawn's death had made national news, as did the wife and three daughters he was leaving behind. When Antonio learned that Nivea was actually Shawn's stepdaughter, he knew that God had made a way for him to finally be reunited with his child. When he heard that she was a basketball star, he made it his mission to recruit her.

That's all that Natasha had left in her to explain to Donte. She was so tired from all that had just transpired. She wanted to go home and cuddle with the baby girl she'd let down.

Donte had his own feelings about the situation. Letting another man raise his daughter because Antonio wasn't man enough to do it on his own was unjustifiable. He'd waited 18 years to be a better man? Donte was convinced that If he really wanted to find her years ago, he would've.

"Let's find Nivea and get you two home," said Donte, grabbing Natasha's hand and their food. "I'll drive this time."

They walked outside to find Nivea sitting next to Antonio in the back seat of his car. Donte scooped Nivea up, long legs and all, and placed her in his own vehicle.

"I'll see you later," Antonio called after her.

He watched them drive off in Donte's vehicle and recalled the evening's events to the forefront of his mind.

Unbeknownst to Natasha and Nivea, Antonio hadn't come back just to introduce himself as Nivea's father. He was also determined to reclaim her mother's heart by any means necessary. He wanted to take them both back home with him, so they could finally be the family he knew he was ready for. That meant squashing whatever she had going on with her former husband's armor bearer.

SHENAE

In 21 days of knowing each other, Shenae and Angelo had shared 13 day-dates, 3 Bible studies, and countless hours of prayer together. And Sheane was, honestly, over the moon. Angelo was everything she didn't know she needed, and the two had done a good job of keeping their relationship strictly platonic. He hadn't even made an attempt to kiss her. But why did she still get butterflies when she saw him or when he called?

"I had a great time at Bible study tonight," Angelo told Shenae as they pulled into her driveway. "You know I have an extra shift tomorrow, so I'll be out of commission."

She looked at him and felt the familiar feeling rising in her gut. Should she kiss him, she wondered. Is that what two people did when they were dating? Was she dating him?

"Oh, you're doing the police detail at that restaurant tonight?" she asked him, not making any moves to leave the car just yet.

"Yes, I'm actually going in tonight," he answered. "I'll call you tomorrow after I get off my regular shift. OK?"

It was her signal to leave the car. Angelo walked around and opened her door and she gave him a farewell kiss on the cheek. Shenae watched him drive off in his car before entering her house. Both he and her gave a sigh of relief that they were taking their time to let God heal their hearts instead of jumping into something.

That night, Shenae lay in her bed and said her prayers a little differently. Angelo was different in the best way she could have imagined. They didn't just talk about God, but he had taken time out to find out her life's passion. She had to think back a long way because, for as long as she could remember, everything that she had ever done was related to church. They talked about Angelo's life as well. He had been married for 10 years before his wife left him. Though he wouldn't elaborate, he did tell Shenae that it was an awful breakup. His life was now dedicated to his kids. Angelo had three boys that ranged in age from 7 to 13 years old. The oldest boy was actually his wife's son from a previous relationship, but Angelo had stepped in for the boy's absent father.

As Shenae looked up at the ceiling in her bedroom, she thought about the last time she'd given herself over to reflection. Since she'd moved into the new condo, she hadn't really taken any time to just think about things. Usually, she spent her lonely nights watching her custom ceiling fan run circles until she fell asleep. She now realized that it mirrored her feelings about her prior marriage. Back then, she was running in circles trying to convince herself that she was happy. And when it first ended, Shenae had literally been at her worst. She was just now coming to terms with the fact that she wasn't to blame for her marriage's demise. But she'd spent the first few months after Leon went away dissecting the failure of her union. She'd purchased and read at least a dozen books detailing how to recover from divorce. But they'd been useless.

When Shenae first met Angelo, she remembered him telling her that it wasn't her fault.

"It is not my fault," she said out loud.

It was the first time that she had said it back to herself. Rising from her spot on the bed, she said it again.

"It is not my fault."

Anxious to tell someone, she picked up the phone and dialed.

"Hey, Shenae. Are you alright?" answered the sleepy voice on the other end.

"Yes, Angelo," she responded. "I know it's late, but I had to tell you thank you."

"You're welcome, I guess," he answered, confused. "What did I do?"

"Thank you for telling me that what happened in my marriage wasn't my fault. I perhaps let some things slip instead of trying to fix what was already broken, but I didn't destroy my marriage."

Shenae had been so happy so share the news that she didn't think about Angelo's work schedule. She looked at the time. 10:30 pm. He was going in to work at midnight.

"That's all, really," Shenae said. "I'll let you get back to sleep before wor—"

"Angelo, who is that calling so late?"

Shenae heard a feminine voice yell from Angelo's side of the phone.

"Oh no, I'm sorry. I didn't think you'd have company. Forgive me," Shenae said, hanging up the phone.

She hadn't waited for him to respond. God had allowed her to see that he was involved with someone, and that she was almost a fool for trusting someone again. She glanced down at her phone to see Angelo calling her back. She sent him to voicemail, but that didn't stop him from calling for the next 30 minutes. Shenae was furious with herself. Yes, she'd told him that she wasn't interested at first and she'd agreed to only be friends, but that didn't stop the twinge of jealousy as she thought about him having late night visitors at his home.

He probably had taken it upon himself to rescue whoever that was in the background. It was very novelesque: gorgeous, formerly broken-hearted man makes it his life mission to pick up women online and mend their broken hearts through coffee and Bible study. Shenae sighed, sensing the writer in her shining through. She had long given up the idea that she would write the next best novel and enjoy her evenings typing away in front of a computer. Suddenly, she felt like writing again for the first time in ten years. There were so many things she wanted to say, but she had no idea where to start. She threw her head back and laughed. Maybe she would write about her life—the rise and fall of her marriage to Leon. She reached for her journal and wrote her daily affirmation.

Dear Journal, My divorce was not my fault.

After that, she drifted off to sleep. She would, of course, probably dream about the gorgeous Angelo. She only hoped that her dreams would be PG. Please Jesus, she thought, let them be PG.

NATASHA

Natasha hadn't slept all night. She had forced her eyes closed after she sent Lynette a text about her evening. It was, by far, the most exhausting day she'd had in along time. She didn't remember much about the ride home from the restaurant last night. She honestly felt numb, besides the comfort of Donte holding her hand in the car and the cool night air hitting her face.

She rolled over in bed to see a fully clothed Donte laying on the recliner in her room. Natasha was sure he didn't get much sleep either. He'd probably been watching over her like a hawk as she tried to rest.

She quietly got up from her bed and went downstairs. She could hear Nivea outside shooting basketball in the early morning hours. Natasha desperately wished she knew what to say to her daughter after the previous night's events. Perhaps she'd just begin with "good morning" and see how the conversation went from there.

But first, she'd need coffee, she thought, walking into the kitchen. She rolled her hand across her neck in response to the strain of pressure she felt. Natasha knew that she was dangerously close to having a massive headache. She hadn't eaten since yesterday morning and she felt like the weight of the world was upon her.

"If you want, I can help you ease some of that tension in your shoulders," she heard Antonio's voice behind her. "I still have magic fingers."

"What are you doing here?" Natasha asked, spinning around and looking at him in her kitchen.

He was standing in the doorway, looking like something out of a magazine. His legs were long and muscular. His chest hadn't changed much with age. He was wearing a cutoff tank and basketball shorts. The whole ensemble was inappropriate and sinful to watch.

"Nivea asked me to come by," he answered. "She said she couldn't sleep."

Natasha just stared at him, taking in his masculinity.

"Listen, I know that things are getting complicated around here," he continued. "And I want you to know that my intention was not to complicate things at all. I came to court you again, to give you all the things that I never had a chance to."

Was this really happening right now? Natasha noticed Antonio taking a few steps toward her and braced herself against the kitchen counter.

"I know that Donte has a thing for you, but what we have is a history," Antonio said, moving toward her again. "We have a daughter, T-Shae. I want to be a part of your life in every way that a man should."

Natasha was stuck. Stuck to the floor, stuck against the counter, just stuck. She was trying her best to recall any scripture that gave her permission to run out of the room. There was a half-naked, fine man talking to her with his veins and muscles bulging as he spoke. Antonio was telling her that he wanted a future with her. She couldn't decide whether she was angry with him for finally realizing she was the one or curious about who they could be if she gave him another chance.

"I'm not going to skirt around how I feel anymore," he told her. "I'm here for Nivea and I'm here for you."

"Listen, Antonio. I am not really in a place to make any decis..."

Before she could answer, he was invading her space. Memories of late nights in his dorm room and dates at the college café were flooding Natasha's mind. This was her first love, a man that she'd loved with every once of her being once. The obvious attraction to him combined with the manly scent of his body was wreaking havoc on her rationale. Natasha looked down to avoid his eyes. She'd melt if she saw them.

"I'm not asking you to decide about us now," he said. "But don't deny that you feel something when I'm this close to you."

She couldn't deny it. She absolutely couldn't deny it. And as he made a move to kiss her, she couldn't deny him.

He grabbed her chin and bent down to meet her lips. Instantly, she was dizzy with the familiarity of the moment. He held her like he used to, his tall frame bending over her small height. With his left hand, he molded himself into her, creating an almost seamless definition. She could feel his reaction to her on her leg. No man besides her late husband had been this close to her in a long time. Even Donte had never had the chance to solicit the groans that were escaping her throat as Antonio captured her lips. Natasha's tongue danced with his down memory lane, but this time he was a man. He wasn't rough and unmanaged; he was sure of what he wanted. It was her. He wanted her.

When he finally broke the kiss and she came down from her tiptoes, Natasha couldn't move. She opened her eyes and waited for him to say something. But he looked just as stunned as she did.

"Am I interrupting something?" Donte asked.

She looked beyond Antonio to see Donte standing in the doorway. Oh no, she thought, had he just witnessed her kiss another man? How was she going to explain all of this?

"Natasha, may I speak with you?" Donte asked, motioning toward the living room.

His blood was boiling, and he wanted to punch a hole in Antonio's head. He had been waiting longer than he wanted for Natasha and now he was forced to watch this guy come from nowhere and swoop in for the steal. This was not the way he had envisioned their future when he'd proposed to Natasha. Donte couldn't do it anymore; he couldn't be waiting in the wing while she lived and he watched. He was done with this.

"Decide," he yelled far above the octave he meant to.

"What?" Natasha asked, unsure of what she was supposed to say.

"Decide what you want right now, Natasha," Donte said again. He was so angry that his eyes were filling with tears. "Decide, because I'm done"

He wouldn't wait another 10 years for her to make up her mind about what she wanted.

"Donte, it's not what you think," Natasha found herself saying something she instantly regretted.

"Oh, I get it. You just wanted to see how much he'd changed since the last time you saw each other. You know, since he left you pregnant," Donte fumed at her. "No, I know it. It took you over a year to kiss me, but then this guy shows up and, in no time at all, you're lip locking with him. Guess you wanted to see if you'd hit the lottery like you did last time with Shawn."

He had crossed the line, bringing Shawn into the conversation, but he was furious.

"What? That's not fair," Natasha yelled back at him.

She was hurt, he could tell. And he knew he'd been the one to hurt her this time. It was too late to tell her that he knew he was wrong, but loving her was making him crazy. Loving her was making him question himself in ways that he'd never imagined. He'd done everything right and had been heartbroken in the end.

"Donte, I know you are angry," she said to him. "And because I love you like a brother, I will forgive that last statement."

"Exactly," he said. And in that moment, he felt the need to grab her and kiss her like he wanted to. He needed to show her. "I'm not your brother, Natasha."

He grabbed her cheeks forcefully and pressed his face into hers, bruising her lips. It was forced and unromantic, nothing like their first kiss had been.

Natasha pushed him off of her, a little offended. Donte threw his hands up and walked toward the door. He needed to leave. Natasha ran behind him, thinking of anything she could do to stop him.

"Donte!"

He turned around. Nothing was calm about him.

"I need you to know what you want, Natasha," he said. "I am not waiting around for you to realize that what you had with him is over, and what you have with me is your future. I won't watch another man court you. I already told you that."

Donte turned to Nivea who had just walked in from outside.

"I love you, Niv. I'll see you later," he said, avoiding her eyes and walking out the front door.

Natasha stared after him as he left. And for the first time in a long time, she felt completely alone.

LYNETTE

Lynette hadn't stop smiling since the romantic night she had shared with Pastor Andre. Not only did he make love to her all night long, but in the morning, he woke her up with kisses and another round of lovemaking in the shower. She loved that they couldn't keep their hands off each other. All the fun had made her tired, but she had so much to do today. Her phone had gone off most of the night with texts from Natasha, and after getting caught up on the chaos, Lynette called for an emergency gathering. The ladies were coming to her house and they had to talk through what was happening.

The ladies were scheduled to arrive in the next 15 minutes, which meant Amauri would probably be there in 10. Lynette ran up the stairs to change into casual attire. She thought to keep her jogging pants on but then remembered how the ladies did casual. A sundress and gladiator sandals would have to do. It was her favorite color, blue, with a red abstract print adorned across the soft fabric. It was a new piece that she'd bought when her new size had forced her to update her wardrobe. At first, she was devastated when she found out she'd become a size 8, but Pastor Andre seemed to love it. All that time she was walking around thinking that as a First Lady, she needed to be a size 4, and he'd wanted her with a little more weight on her. She laughed as she slipped on the dress, thinking how much the new weight seemed to have paid off in the bedroom.

"I was wondering if you were going to keep those sweats on," Pastor Andre said.

Lynette looked over her shoulder. She thought that her giant was sleeping, but he fooled her. He had been watching her the whole time. Andre had gotten a late start to his day since the DNA test had been rescheduled for a later date. She stood in the doorway to the closet, looking at him sprawled on his stomach. He was so sexy, Lynette thought. His muscles peeked from underneath the sheets, just begging to be touched.

"Honey, are you going to the church today? Don't we have outreach?" Lynette asked, her mind slipping back into First Lady mode.

"Yeah," her husband answered, stretching in the sheets. "I'm going in about an hour. I have a prayer breakfast with Bishop Paden, and then we will head over."

He paused, as if he had something on his mind.

"What's up, babe?" she asked, looking at him through the mirror while she accessorized.

"I was going to wait until tonight to talk to you about this, but I want us to go on a fast this week. I know that I have to preach Sunday, so I need time to get into my Word and study."

Lynette loved when Andre put the house on a mandatory fast. They even let the kids get involved, and they would all talk about the things they wanted God to do. Benny and Ivory didn't take it seriously yet; their expectation was always ice cream before dinner.

"Of course, baby," she said.

Slipping out of First Lady mode, she turned around to face her husband.

"Not to distract you," Lynette started, "but how many licks does it take to get to the center of your lollipop?"

She went over to the bed and invited herself into Andre's space. He leaned back to hold her in his arms.

"Well, we'll just have to let you find out, lady."

"Sounds like a challenge I'm up for," Lynette said, kissing her husband's neck. "Since soon, I won't be able to touch you for a whole week."

"We don't have to give *that* up, do we?" he asked, pulling her closer to him.

First Ladies Club: Rocks, Rings and Resurrections

"No sir, we have the rest of our lives to make love, " she laughed, pulling away. "We need direction, and that requires us to be in a place where we can hear God with no distractions."

Andre pushed aside the covers in response to reveal that he was still naked in bed. He pulled her on top of him.

"Babe!" she squealed. "I have guests coming. We can't."

"I know, but when they leave, it's on girl," he said, placing kisses on her fully clothed body.

As Lynette got up from the bed, Andre goofed off in front of her to show her what she was missing. Still nude, he posed, flexing his muscles for her.

"I think you missed your calling for Chippendales," she said, laughing at her husband's lighter side. She knew what they were about to go through was bound to take a toll on him. She was glad that Andre was able to let it all go and be silly with her. She almost wished she didn't have to run off to her meeting.

They both heard the doorbell ring. Lynette ran downstairs to answer, winking at her husband before she left him.

She opened her front door to find Natasha. Her friend was dressed in the most horrible thing she'd ever seen her in. She wearing all black with a pair of oversized shades and her hair was pulled back into a messy ponytail.

"Are you drunk, Natasha?" Lynette asked, unable to hold back her disgust.

"No, I am not drunk. I've had a bad couple of days," Natasha said, walking into the house and plopping down on the couch.

"Sorry," Lynette apologized, looking at Natasha as if she was some sort of science project. "You just look…"

"Thanks," Natasha said when she saw Lynette couldn't find the words.

Lynette watched as Natasha removed her glasses. She couldn't imagine it was possible that her sister could look any worse than she did, but her eyes were bloodshot red and the bags underneath looked like they were holding rocks.

"You want to talk about it?" Lynette asked.

"Not really. I just want to make it through the rest of the day without crying or kissing anyone," Natasha said, stuffing her shades into her bag a little too hard.

That statement, of course, immediately got Lynette's attention.

"What?" Lynette asked. "Kissing who? You can't say you don't want to talk about it after you say something like that."

Before Natasha could explain, the doorbell rang again. Sure that it was Amauri, Lynette opened it to find a glowing Shenae instead.

It was as if she was meeting her for the first time. Shenae had on khaki shorts and a form-fitting shirt with wedge sandals. Looking this stranger up and down, Lynette could see that Shenae's toes were painted bright orange. She was wearing her hair down today, with her natural curls cascading around her pear shaped face. She looked rested and calmer than Lynette had seen her in months.

"Girl, what's gotten into you? You look amazing!"

Grinning from ear to ear, Shenae instantly knew that she had chosen the right outfit. She wanted to wear something that reflected how she felt on the inside. She had gone to sleep the night before finally free of her past and woke up feeling like her life was about to take a promising turn. She'd received the strangest email from her attorney telling her that the monies that were frozen in her joint account with Leon had been suddenly unfrozen. Shenae knew that her lawyer had been fighting on her behalf so that she could gain control of her money again. In disbelief, she'd called her bank and was cited a balance that almost made her fall from her seat.

It had taken over a year of waiting, but finally, things were looking up for Shenae. And so she treated herself to a few pieces that morning to spice up her wardrobe. The clothes she owned just didn't fit her mood anymore. Her wealth was restored and, more than anything, her confidence had returned. She was glad she had already thanked Angelo for all he'd helped her through, and even more glad that she discovered that he had another woman. Shenae considered herself lucky to have found out about his philandering ways before she thought about a relationship. All they had was coffee and she had let herself already start thinking about them in a relationship. She chastened herself for the misjudgment.

"I just had a great morning," responded Shenae, entering the house. "I can't wait to share my testimony."

She stopped mid-stride upon seeing Natasha.

"What in the...?"

"I know how I look, Shenae," responded Natasha from the couch. "I just need us to sit down and talk about anything that is not my life."

"Your text is the reason I called this meeting," Lynette reminded. "We're your sisters. We're here for you, no matter who you've been kissing."

"Kissing?!" exclaimed Shenae. "Again?"

Natasha groaned and hung her head in defeat.

"Where is Amauri?" she asked, going through her phone to check for any missed calls. Antonio had called her 10 times today and Nivea had sent her a text asking to spend the night at a friend's house. Nothing from Amauri. And furthermore, nothing from Donte.

Natasha called Amauri's phone twice and was sent to voicemail each time. It was very unlike her to not answer the phone.

"Andre, can you bring my cell down?" Lynette called up to her husband.

Andre came downstairs with her phone in hand. He had put on a fresh shirt and slacks. His bowtie hung unfastened around his collar.

"What's going on?" he asked.

"Have you heard from Bishop Paden?" she asked him, dialing the bishop's phone. It also went straight to voicemail.

"No babe, I haven't," Andre answered, pulling his phone from his pocket to check for a missed call. "We made plans for a meeting in an hour so. Once I meet him, I'll call you."

Pastor Andre looked around the room at the two Deborah's Daughters sitting in his living room. He couldn't help but to fix his eyes on the normally polished and put together Natasha.

"Oh, hey ladies," he greeted them, trying not to stare at her.

"We haven't heard from Amauri, and she's always on time. Bishop's phone is going to voicemail. Something's is wrong," commented Lynette.

"Honey, maybe they slept in like us," Pastor Andre said with a sly grin, causing Lynette to turn red.

"Babe, this is serious. Somethings wrong."

"Look, if Bishop doesn't show up to our meeting, then we will worry. God has them. I'll see you later," Pastor Andre said, kissing her on the forehead and gesturing bye to the ladies.

Moments after Andre left, the room was filled with prayer for Amauri and Bishop Paden's safety. Suddenly, the doorbell rang, startling everyone.

"I hope that's her," said Lynette, running to open it.

A familiar face dressed in a police uniform was standing on her porch. His tag read "Garcia."

"Good afternoon, ma'am," he said, removing his officer cap.

"Don't I know you?" she asked him.

"The coffee bar, right?" he answered. "You're Shenae's friend."

SHENAE

Upon hearing her name and hearing Angelo's voice, Shenae rushed to the door.

"Angelo, right?" Lynette was saying to him, recalling their first meeting at the café. He was more handsome than she remembered, probably because he was wearing a badge and a gun. She guessed it was true what they said about men in uniforms; she just happened to prefer her man wearing a robe and not a "protect and serve" plate on his chest.

Lynette turned to find Shenae peering over her shoulder.

"I'll leave you two alone," she said, returning to her living room.

"Angelo, what are you doing here?" Shenae asked.

The two hadn't spoken since she'd heard the other woman in his house. Had he somehow followed her here?, she thought to herself.

"Hey, I didn't realize you'd be here," he started. "Um, I found this couple on the side of the road and I recognized the wife as one of your friends."

"On the side of the road?" Shenae asked in horror. "What? Oh, God, no."

"It's nothing like that," he assured her. "They asked me to bring them here."

Angelo turned and waved his arms, gesturing for Amauri and Bishop Paden to come out of his squad car.

"Their tire popped, and I saw them on the side of the road," he informed Shenae as the couple walked up the steps to Lynette's house.

Shenae went to hug her friend's neck.

"We knew something was wrong," she told Amauri. "You're always five minutes early."

Amauri laughed as they all stepped inside to offer relief to the ladies waiting inside.

"Is Pastor Andre here?" Bishop Paden asked Lynette as he gave her a hug.

"No, he went down to the diner to meet you for the prayer lunch," she told him. "I'll call him and tell him you're ok."

Shenae looked back at Angelo waiting in the doorway.

"Excuse me for a moment?" she found herself asking for permission. "I'll be right back."

"I hope you tell that woman you talked about her the entire ride," Bishop Paden called over his shoulder to Angelo, causing everyone to laugh.

All things work together for the good, Shenae remembered. She closed the door behind her to speak to Angelo on the porch.

"You look beautiful today," Angelo said, unintentionally staring at her from head to toe.

He wasn't trying to scare her off with romantic gestures just yet, but she looked radiant. After last night, however, he was unsure of how well he may be received. Angelo had been in God's ear constantly about his relationship with this woman. He valued their friendship and had been coming up with ways to explain the female Shenae had heard over the phone.

"Thanks," Shenae said, receiving the compliment and interrupting his thoughts. "Shouldn't you be going back to work?"

Shenae wanted to end things quietly with Angelo without the pressure of her friends challenging her decision or asking too many questions. She'd been the first one to question Natasha's motives when she came to them about Donte. Shenae regretted it now because she knew her friend deserved to be happy, but she wasn't open to receiving that same type of scrutiny.

"I'd rather be here with you," he said, swiftly dodging her defense mechanism. "I think we need to talk about what you think you may have heard."

"No need to explain," Shenae said. "I blame myself for calling you at such a late hour. It was completely out of line."

She was trying to shut Angelo down before the butterflies took over or before he said something that put her under his spell.

"If I'd known that you were otherwise occupied, then I would not have called you anyway," she finished.

"The voice you heard was my sister," Angelo said calmly, throwing Shenae completely off guard. "My sister, Kenya. We've only just reconnected. My father didn't tell me about her until I was an adult."

The shadow of embarrassment soared over Shenae as she listened to him tell the story of how his sister was helping him recover from the financial strain of divorce. Not only did finalizing his separation cost him thousands in lawyer fees and other legal costs, but his ex-wife also ended up robbing him of his assets and placing him on child support. After two years of barely making it on his own, Angelo's father came clean about his half-sister who lived in Atlanta.

"My sister has been a Godsend," he said, also admitting that he never told Shenae about her because he was embarrassed to be living with his sister. "I am financially recovering, though, so I don't want you to think that I am a dead beat. I pay rent, and I take care of my children. They are my top priority."

"Wow, I'm so sorry," Shenae said, apologizing for her wrongful judgment. "I have to tell you that I thought the voice I heard was from a female friend that you were entertaining."

Angelo threw his head back in laughter at her confession. It caused more embarrassment to wash over her again.

"Oh, Shenae," he said, noticing her discomfort. "How am I entertaining other ladies if I'm always hanging out with you?"

He ran his hands through his thick black hair, causing another emotion to spike Shenae in the gut. She wondered what his hair felt like, what it smelled like, how it would feel if she ran her fingers through it…

"Lawd Jesus," she muttered. "Think on things that are lovely and things that are of good report."

This boy was bound to get her in trouble, she thought, washing away all impure feelings. She'd have to begin a fast or something to shut this down. She would not be the woman in the church that had intimate visions of a man that was not her husband.

"Hey, you ok?" Angelo asked, having heard her scripture recital.

He softly placed his hand on her shoulder, hoping it would calm her. His mind was almost as much of a wreck as hers.

"Oh, I'm fine. I just had a moment," Shenae began. "Um, I'd love to meet your sister. You should invite her to Amauri's going away party on Saturday."

"I will do that," he said, his dimples alerting the hairs on the back of her neck to stand up. "So does that mean you'd like me to escort you to the party?"

"I do believe that would be great. I think it would be a great restart to our friendship," Shenae answered, stressing that things were still strictly platonic between them. Now, if only she could tell the fire that she thought had gone out inside of her to stop flickering.

NATASHA

Inside Lynette's house, Natasha and the other ladies listened to Bishop Paden tell the story of how he and Amauri met. It was obvious to everyone in the room that their love, interracial or not, was the real thing.

Natasha felt bad in that moment that she'd always doubted Amauri's motives simply because she was a white woman. Her experience years ago with Antonio had left her scarred and unable to see that love wasn't predicated on color. What Antonio did to her all those years ago had nothing to do with color and everything to do with him being unable to step up as a man.

"Amauri, I am sorry," Natasha found herself interrupting Bishop Paden midsentence. "About how I treated you when we first met."

Natasha could feel everyone's attention shifting to her, and suddenly she felt like the woman in all black with the wild hair. But, she needed Amauri's forgiveness.

"Looking at the two of you together makes me feel horrible about what I thought," Natasha continued, grabbing Amauri's hands. "And I know that no matter where you go, the Lord will be magnified and the hearts of men changed. I pray that God sends me someone I can love just the same way."

She leaned in to give Amauri a hug and kiss her on the cheek.

It was a heartfelt moment for the Daughters, and it warmed Bishop Paden's heart to see that someone else saw what he saw in his wife. She was so beautiful, he thought, inside and out. Paden dreaded the secrets that he hadn't shared with her. She was so trusting and so giving, and he knew that, in turn, he must give her more. But he didn't know how to be completely honest with her just yet.

"Thank you sis," Amauri said, receiving Natasha's embrace. Suddenly, she extended her hands out to grab Natasha's face and speak over her life.

"There is a place that God wants to take you This place is where you will not only see the forgiveness of God but also feel it," Amauri began. "You have held on to some things from your past that have kept you in a state of hiding and waiting. God desires to use you in a way that you have not imagined."

The room had fallen into complete silence. God had the floor and was using Amauri to speak to His daughter.

"Your title as First lady hid you," Amauri continued. She could feel Natasha's tears wetting her fingers. "But I declare that the covers have been stripped and the veil has been lifted. God is exposing you for His greater good."

When the Word for her had ended, Natasha opened her eyes to find everyone smiling at her. She was glad that she had friends that encouraged her and didn't judge her based on the state of her life. Being this vulnerable in front of others was not her style, but it had become common after Shawn's death. She had always been put together and she did everything because she wanted her daughter to be healthy and happy. Natasha had given up her dreams because she wanted Nivea to have hers. Her happiness had even played second to her husband's for such a long time, but Natasha hoped the words that Amauri was speaking over her life would be just what she needed to move forward.

"Thanks everybody," she said, as Shenae and Angelo entered the house.

"Looks like we missed something special," Shenae commented, seeing Natasha's smile shine through her ruined makeup.

"I was about to say the same to you," Natasha responded, noticing that everything was back to normal between the two.

"I've invited Angelo and his sister to Amauri and Bishop's going away party," said Shenae. "I figure two more can't hurt."

"That only brings the total to 152," Lynette laughed. "The house will be packed. I'll call the caterer and make the changes."

Lynette had spent the morning on the phone with the caterers, the florists, and their wonderful event planner from Eventista Productions, Ny Bowen. Lynette needed Nye there to set up beforehand because she had the appointment with her husband and Harriet to finally get the DNA test out of the way. Hopefully, the party would go off without a hitch.

Amauri and Bishop Paden were delighted that their friends thought enough of them to pull of a party of the magnitude they were describing. They were so blessed and both would miss the bond that they'd shared here with the Daughters.

"Angelo, would you mind driving me to meet Pastor Andre?" Bishop Paden asked. "I know we've asked too much of you already."

"Of course," responded Angelo, pulling his car keys from his pocket. "I'm off for the day anyway. I'll see you later, Shenae?"

"I hope so," she said, heading with them toward the door.

As she watched everyone head out, Natasha saw that Antonio was calling her again. Instead of ignoring him, as she'd done all day, she answered.

"Hey, I can't talk right now. Can you come by the house later?" she asked, hugging Lynette goodbye and heading to her car.

"Mom, where've you been?" Nivea asked as her mother walked in the house later than usual.

Natasha hadn't expected her daughter to be home.

"I went to the spa," a refreshed and rejuvenated Natasha answered. She needed a pick-me-up and, more than ever, she needed to stop wallowing in her bad decisions and just deal with life head on.

"I thought you were staying at a friend's," she said, removing her pedicure sandals and slipping her feet into her favorite slippers.

"I was, but then Coach Tony told me we were having family night," her daughter responded, pointing toward Antonio coming out of the kitchen with a bowl of popcorn.

"Family night, anyone?" Antonio asked, playfully holding the popcorn out for Natasha to taste.

When Natasha asked him to come over, it was so the two of them could talk. She hadn't expected to make it a family affair.

"We already picked a movie," Nivea told her mom, flashing a smile that told Natasha she was genuinely happy.

"Family night it is then," Natasha said, joining her daughter on the couch.

Her long-legged daughter tucked herself into her mother's arm and Natasha rubbed her hair. Antonio sat at the other end of the couch with Nivea's toes tucked under his legs. As the movie played, Natasha caught Antonio staring at her a few times. She looked at him.

This is nice, he mouthed.

She smiled in response and kissed Nivea on her forehead. She had to admit that it was.

About an hour into the film, Nivea drifted off to sleep and was snoring louder than the TV.

"Sweetie," Natasha said, nudging her awake. "Go to bed. Mommy will see you in the morning."

She helped her giant baby to get up and pointed her toward the stairs.

"Okay Mom," Nivea said, turning back toward the couch. "Goodnight Dad."

As she heard her daughter thump around upstairs, Natasha wanted to believe that what she'd just heard was just a slip of the tongue from Nivea. But the truth was that Antonio was her father. She couldn't deny that truth anymore, nor could she deny that there was still a fire between them that hadn't been resolved yet. Natasha couldn't distinguish if she was just in heat or if this was really repressed love. It was something she was willing to take a chance and figure it out, especially if it meant that Nivea would be happy. Of course, Donte was still an unresolved topic for her, but right now she had to consider what was best for her daughter. And after seeing Nivea smile like that tonight, maybe a family was exactly what she needed.

"How was your evening?" Antonio asked, rising from his place on the couch to kiss her cheek. "You look great."

Natasha knew that he was using that moment as an excuse to get closer to her on the couch but she didn't fight it.

"Thanks. It's good to see you," she admitted. "I know we have a lot to talk about, but instead of hashing that out tonight, let's just watch something on TV. Save the talking for later. Deal?"

"Deal," he said, pulling Natasha into his arm and grabbing the remote.

"Hey!" she exclaimed playfully, reaching to get the remote from his hand.

He held it above his head, and as she lunged toward his long arms, they ended up face-to-face on the couch. Antonio pulled back. He surrendered and gave her the remote. He wanted her, but he wanted her the right way. He wanted her the way that Donte did, free of uncertainty. The chemistry between them was undeniable, but he wanted to make sure that it was authentic this time. It had been 18 years; he had so much ground to make up for. Antonio swore that he wouldn't mess it up by seducing her.

SHENAE

Angelo and Shenae had no idea what time it was, but they'd watched the sun go down side-by-side from the back porch of her home. They were natural together, laughing at each other and sharing embarrassing stories from the past. She couldn't believe she was having so much fun with a man who wasn't married to her. She felt a twinge of guilt spending time with another man but quickly shunned away the emotion.

My marriage is over and it is not my fault, she reminded herself. It caused the feeling to leave as quickly as it had come.

"Hey, are you alright? You phased out on me for a second," Angelo smiled, placing his hand over hers.

Shenae was surprised by how the small gesture didn't make her nervous this time. She could tell that Angelo was a man who believed in the art of touch. Since they'd sat down outside, he had touched her eleven times. She had counted; eleven times their skin had touched, eleven times her inner woman alerted her to calm down. She could hear the phone inside her house ringing, but she wasn't ready for Angelo to even sense it might have been time to leave.

"I'm fine, sorry," she responded. "I was just thinking that you touch me a lot."

Shenae instantly covered her mouth. She was embarrassed that it came out the way it did. She was glad that it was dark outside now he couldn't see how red she was turning.

"I'm sorry if it offends you," he said. "If it bothers you, I'll try to stop."

"No, it's fine. I promise," Shenae assured.

She reached over this time and initiated the touch. They were like teenagers fumbling through a first date. But it wasn't a first date, she reminded herself. They were just two friends getting to know each other. The fluttering in her stomach said otherwise. She looked at him looking back at her and felt the butterflies float free again. The feeling caused her to cover her mouth with her hands in laughter.

"I love your smile. Stop hiding it from me," Angelo said. He moved her hands from her face and found her trying to turn from his gaze. Shenae never thought about the beauty of her smile. It was trademark for her; she was the athletic, middle-aged woman with the gap. She was ok with it but often found herself covering her mouth in shyness.

"Thanks. I like yours too," Shenae said.

This time, she took full advantage to touch the side of his face with the palm of her hand. She could tell it was late in the day because the prickles of his face were beginning to peep through his soft skin. Again, she wondered if she touched his hair, how soft it would be. She wouldn't do it now, but one day, maybe.

When Shenae finally looked down, she saw Angelo's face growing closer to hers. She'd known a long time ago that if a man was this close, he was probably about to kiss her. Instantly, she panicked. A kiss would change everything. Besides, she didn't even think she knew how to kiss anymore. She hadn't kissed a man in so long. Would he want to kiss her sweetly? Or would he want to plunge into her mouth with all that he was? How would she respond? Every emotion possible went through her mind as the space between them closed. Instinctively, her lips puckered in wait. But instead, she felt his lips on her cheek.

"It's getting late. I should go," Angelo said. "My sister will get worried. We'll see you at the going away party tomorrow. She can't wait to meet you."

He stood to his feet and held his hands out to pull a disappointed Shenae up from the step.

"I'm glad you two can make it tomorrow," said Shenae, thinking of anything to say to hold onto the moment longer. "And, um, sorry again for overreacting earlier."

Angelo thought it was cute the way she rocked back and forth when she was nervous. She'd bite the corner of her lip and her eyes would do this weird thing when she talked. He was watching her do it now. She was adorable.

He'd listened to Shenae tell him stories about her mother's flower shop and her two boys. The way that God had touched her life made him think she was invincible. She'd been through some of the worst storms in her life, and she'd survived them all. There were pains that he could tell she didn't like to bring up. Her voice would tremble a little, and he'd have to assure her that the space between them was safe. He wanted to tell her, though, that she didn't need to be brave for him. He knew that the journey ahead of them would be hard if they decided to remain just friends. The two of them were clearly attracted to each other and could chat for hours together as if they'd been friends forever.

"Well…bye," Shenae finally said.

"Bye Nae," Angelo responded, realizing he hadn't heard a word of her rambling just then. He kissed her on the forehead, wishing he could kiss her lips, and turned to leave.

"Bye," she told him.

The last man to call her "Nae" had been Leon. She wasn't ready for that.

"Angelo," she called after him. He'd almost reached his car. "…I need a favor."

"Anything."

"I need you to find a new nickname for me," she shrugged, hoping he wouldn't ask her to go into detail.

Angelo took the hint.

"I was already thinking of all the nicknames I could give you," he told her. "Let's discuss tomorrow, bonita amiga."

Shenae giggled. She hadn't giggled in a long time. It was kind of embarrassing, but she didn't mind. He had just called her "beautiful friend." She could get used to that.

"Good night," she said, waiting for him to get in his car again. They stood staring at each other.

"I'm waiting to make sure that you are in the house, safe and sound," Angelo informed her.

That smile, those eyes, Shenae thought to herself. It was truly a lethal combination.

She felt herself smiling a little too hard as she went inside and closed the door behind her. She slid against it like a woman half her age. She felt it. The "it" that kept women up at night, that made them draw hearts and butterflies in their notebooks. She honestly didn't even know she was capable of feeling all of this.

Her house phone rang for the fifth time that night. No doubt the calls were from Leon, but she wasn't going to let him ruin her evening. Shenae walked upstairs, checked her email to see if

Lynette had sent her any updates regarding the going away party, then climbed in her pajamas. She couldn't wait to relive the past hours she'd had in her dreams.

Her cell phone chimed, alerting her of a text. She reached for it from her place under the covers. It was Angelo.

Goodnight, Beautiful Warrior. Until tomorrow. You are in my prayers and thoughts.

Was she actually kicking the sheets and screaming into her pillow? Yes! Shenae liked a man. And she would not apologize for it.

NATASHA

Natasha woke up to the sound of her daughter running into her room.

"Mom, wake up! You promised we'd go shopping today."

Her teenager was about to jump on her bed until she saw that the sheets were covered in old photo albums. Natasha and Antonio had stayed up half the night reminiscing. And when he'd asked to see pictures of Nivea as a baby, one photo turned into a million.

The night ended with Antonio confessing his love for Natasha. He'd told her that, over the years, he'd never stopped loving her. Now, he wanted them to be a family for Nivea, and he wanted to give Natasha the life of love and affection she admitted she'd been missing all this time.

"Nivea, I'm sleepy," Natasha said, sitting up. "Antonio slept downstairs. Can you two just go alone? Wouldn't that be better?"

She reached and cupped the side of her beautiful daughter's face.

"Baby, are you wearing lip gloss?" Natasha asked, noticed her daughter's lips were more pink than usual. "And when did you take your braids out?"

"Yeah, umm, I wanted to try something new," Nivea said, touching her hair, which was in a twistout from the braids.

"I like it," Natasha complimented her daughter. "Shenae wore hers like that the other day."

"Um…I was thinking we all could go shopping today," started Nivea. "Me, you, and Coach Tony. Is that ok?"

Natasha could see her daughter's anticipation for a positive response.

"If he's up for it," Natasha responded.

"Already asked him!" exclaimed Nivea, bolting out of the room to finish getting ready. "He said yes."

Natasha laughed and sent a grateful prayer up to God that Nivea had taken Antonio's arrival well and hadn't resorted to self-cutting or hard drugs. She got out of bed and looked at her huge king-sized palace. She noticed she still slept on one side. It was a lonely realization, but she had to admit that she missed companionship.

The smell of hazelnut coffee awakened her thoughts and caused her to migrate downstairs to the kitchen. Antonio was there with his shirt off and a pair of basketball shorts on. While his back was turned toward her, she caught herself licking her lips at the deliciousness of him. What was going through her mind could never be considered godly. She'd be sure to repent later.

Natasha flashed back to the last time they'd made love in college. He'd been younger then, and inexperienced, but he took his time with her. She could laugh now at how awkward he was when he first went down to taste her. She'd winced in pain at his attempt to follow the directions his teammates gave him on how to please her. To her, for some reason, it was sweet and cute. Today, she thought, she'd bet that he knew how to make love to her. He'd know how to please her.

"Jesus, please help me," Natasha whispered a little too loudly.

Antonio turned around. He smiled at her, revealing every tooth in his mouth.

"Good morning beautiful," he said.

Natasha willed her body to stay still. She would not run to him, kiss him senseless, and devour him along with the eggs and bacon he was making. She'd have to remember that as much as she wanted to have the right family for her daughter, she also wanted to do what God wanted her to do. She wanted to break the habit of being more concerned with what everyone else thought about her than what God thought. She'd been thinking about Antonio and Donte, trying to make a decision about which man she'd choose, when the one that was most important was the one that gave His life for her soul.

"Good morning, Antonio," she answered him.

"Breakfast will be ready in a few," he told her.

Natasha stayed silent, still in her thoughts.

"Can I ask you a question?" she finally said.

"Of course. What's up?"

"Why did you really come back?" Natasha asked. "We are so different than we were back then. And now you're here, back in my life, I don't understand."

He turned around again to face her. His face was calm.

"I'm back because I know that what I did all those years ago was wrong, Natasha," he said. "I just want an opportunity to reconnect with you."

"Am I supposed to just forget what happened though?" she frowned at him. "I'm supposed to just give you another chance? A chance to hurt me like you did before."

He could tell that the last words hurt Natasha to say. Last night, when he'd spilled his heart to her, she'd been silent in response. But he knew that they needed to deal with the reality that he'd been gone from her life for so long. He needed to give her more than an apology to mend what he'd broken.

He turned the eyes of the stove off and walked over to her.

"I can never change what I did," he said. "I can never truly replace the years that I wasn't in your life, but what I can say is that I am no longer that man. I have never forgotten what we meant to each other, Natasha, and I want to make things right with us."

Antonio gestured upstairs to where Nivea was.

"I want the family that we always talked about," he continued. "I want to still be your Superman. Remember when you used to call me that?"

"Antonio, honestly, with you here so frequently, I can't really think straight," Natasha said.

She looked at the stove. Breakfast for three would've been lovely, especially with their family trip to the mall to follow. "I just think you need to go back to your hotel."

"Ok," he responded, a little confused. "What about the mall and the party later?"

"We'll meet you there," she said, squeezing his hand and making her way toward the stairs. "I'm going to go up and let Nivea know the food is ready. You can let yourself out."

Natasha retreated into her room. Moments later, she heart the soft rumble of an engine. She sighed, relived. She passed the test. All this time, God had placed in front of her a task that she was trying to fight inside by herself. She should've been leaning on Him instead for the answers. When he'd mentioned her nickname for him, she laughed on the inside. The reality that he thought she still needed someone to be her superman was ludicrous. God was her savior. There would be no man that could replace who God was in her life. Somewhere along the way, she'd forgotten that.

She walked into her closet and pushed past all her First Lady attire. Kneeling with her prayer shawl over her head, she prayed. She asked God whose life she could change by sharing her testimony of everything she'd been through. He'd chosen her to go through it for a reason. Her tears were real as she saw the hearts of God's women around the world struggling in the same pain she had. Fatherless children around the world had been betrayed and their mothers, like Natasha, had tried to replace those fathers time and time again. She then asked God for forgiveness and the strength to help forgive herself so she'd be able to tell her story.

LYNETTE

On the morning of Bishop Paden and Amauri's going away party, Lynette and Pastor Andre were spending some alone time with their kids. In an hour or so, the two would venture to the hospital to meet the boy who could be his son. Lynette was nervous, but Andre was her pillar of strength. She wasn't sure how she would respond to seeing Harriet for the first time.

After an hour of fun and games with Benny and Ivory, Pastor Andre signaled to his wife that it was time. They had a schedule to keep and this was first on their agenda. The car ride there was quiet, but they held hands. It was a signal from Lynette that she was not leaving him. She'd even prayed silently the entire time, asking God to give her husband strength to endure what was necessary. Then she prayed for herself. She prayed that she would be the woman of God he needed her to be and not regress to the woman that God had delivered her from. Lynette learned that the key to being a true woman of God was honesty. She was honest to God about her shortcomings. She sent a vague group text to the ladies, asking them to keep her in prayer this morning. She still hadn't told them about her situation.

As they pulled into the parking deck, a hopeful Lynette finished her prayer. Getting out of the car, she felt the chill of the air against her skin and blamed it for the goosebumps traveling up her arm.

"Sweetheart, we will be okay," Pastor Andre said, helping her out of the vehicle.

His eyes were also filled with hope. She'd noticed that he hadn't eaten since early the day before. She assumed that he was fasting and thanked God for total restoration in his gifts and abilities. Looking at how strong he looked now, compared to two years ago, and it warmed her heart. She stood up and straightened his tie.

"We sure will," she told him, planting a kiss on his lips.

"Why are you smiling, First lady?" Pastor Andre asked her.

"I'm just admiring how good my man of God looks," she responded, grabbing his hand so they could make their way into the hospital. "I am so proud of what God is doing in you and I'm even more proud that he chose me to help you become it."

As they stepped off the elevator on the assigned floor, Lynette spotted Harriet at the end of the hallway.

The woman she used to despise spotted them and came toward them. She outstretched her arms to give Pastor Andre a hug and Lynette graciously stepped in front of him. She offered Harriet her hand in salutation, her newfound calm and sweet spirit shining through.

"Good morning, Harriet," she said.

It wasn't as if she thought that Harriet still had a chance with her husband, but she didn't want to be too careful. Harriet didn't look as good as she had four years ago. It was funny what can happen with time, Lynette thought to herself. She looked much older, and her eyes carried the weight of guilt and condemnation. Condemnation was the devil's greatest weapon against people who strived after the things of God. Instead of feeling angry or mad at the woman that slept with her husband all those years ago, she again felt sorry for her.

Lynette pulled her hand away and gave Harriet a hug. The woman crumbled into her arms and Lynette felt the weight of four years worth of strife melt away in her arms.

"Harriet, I forgive you," she told her again, and this time she meant it fully.

"Thank you so much. You don't know what that means to me to hear you say that," Harriet said, her voice shaken and distraught.

She pulled away and looked at Harriet. She'd still never understand what happened between this woman and her husband, but the past was the past.

"Now," Lynette said, rubbing Harriet's shoulder, "let's see your baby boy." The nurse took a blood sample from Pastor Andre, letting him know that it would take about 24 hours to find out if he was a match. Afterward, Pastor Andre handled Harriet and her baby, Levi, as he would any sick family needing healing. He knelt and prayed with the family and then they left. Lynette decided at the last minute to stay out from the hospital room because she just wasn't ready to see the boy. She wasn't ready to look for the similarities between the boy and her husband.

When Lynette returned home, she thought she was fine. Pastor Andre had rushed to the downstairs bathroom and left her in the foyer of their house. She sat on the edge of her couch and the realization that her husband may have fathered another child hit her. Lynette sat there, crying for Benny and Ivory and for the little boy she'd refused to meet earlier that day.

When Pastor Andre rounded the corner of the house, he heard his wife's cries. Her hands were trembling, and she held them close to her body to comfort herself. He prayed over her heart and didn't let her go.

"Thank you so much for being brave today," he whispered into her ear. Next, he carried her upstairs and ran her a hot bath. She lay still in the warm water, letting it wash away all her fears.

"I love you," she told him. "So much.""

I love you too, Lynn," he responded. "You and Benny and Ivory are my life."

SHENAE

The day of the party, Shenae woke up to text messages and emails from the event coordinator and guests. They all seemed urgent, but Shenae seemed to float on a cloud all morning. For her, 5 p.m. couldn't come soon enough; she'd be seeing Angelo again. She daydreamed that he'd see her from across the room and she'd glide toward him, eager for his touch. Just a touch, though, she assured herself. She was trying her best to keep things holy and pure. Shenae had been fasting and she'd even chosen not to watch certain things on TV and remove herself from conversations that were more than she could handle. As a woman of God trying to live a life acceptable to Him, she had to make sacrifices to remain righteous. She understood that if God was going to bless her with the type of man that she deserved, it would come only after she tamed the nuisance that was her flesh.

The drive to the venue was peaceful. She was hopeful in knowing God was restoring her and resurrecting her from the ashes of her heartbreak.

As Shenae walked into the venue, both excitement and sadness overwhelmed her. The party setup was a stunning sight, but the reality that Amauri was moving made her feel cheerless. She joined the event planner, Ny, who was instructing the staff to move things around.

"This looks perfect," she told her, gazing at the chandeliers overhead. "Amauri and Bishop will love it."

"It was my pleasure," responded Ny with her iPad in hand. "How have you been? I haven't seen you in quite some time."

"I'm well, thanks. It has been a long road, but He made me for it," Shenae told her.

"Amen to that!" Ny gave her a high-five. "Everything is in place, and we are ready to send off the couple in style. Now if you'll excuse me, I need to make sure that dinner is almost prepared. "

Shenae watched Nyasia walk toward the back of the room into the kitchen. She continued to take in the ambiance of the grand hall, noticing that lilies, Amauri's favorite flowers, were everywhere. They honestly made the room come alive; it smelled heavenly. But today was not about pomp and circumstance, she reminded herself. It was about sending their friend off today. She looked toward the doors to see that they guests had begun to arrive. From all the "oohs" and "aahs" she could hear from them, she considered the work a job well done. To her right, Shenae could hear marvelous jazz notes fill the adjoining greenhouse where the dance floor was located.

"Let the fun begin," she said to herself, smiling.

"Hey Shenae," she heard a voice behind her call. "You look magnificent."

It was Natasha, accompanied by a tall, muscular man she was guessing was Antonio. He looked quite dapper in just a pair of slacks with a button up top and bowtie. Natasha, the sassier one of the bunch, was dressed in a knee-length, fitted turquoise dress with beautiful black lace covering. She'd paired the classy dress with strappy sandals.

"Hey Natasha," Shenae said, greeting her friend.

In moving to hug her, she noticed a new addition on her finger. She grabbed Natasha's hand and gasped.

"Wait, is that a ring?!"

NATASHA

She died a little on the inside when Shenae noticed the new rock weighing down her hand.

"Excuse us please, Antonio," she said, hurriedly pulling Shenae into a corner in the grand room.

"You, my dear, have got a lot of explaining to do," Shenae said as they rushed off.

"I don't know what to tell you Shenae, it just happened," Natasha tried to explain. "Like an hour ago."

Natasha told Shenae the story of how a trip to the mall had ended in more complication than she could take right now. She and Nivea had met Antonio at the mall after she'd asked him to leave her house. After hours of looking through shoes and clothes with the two of them, Antonio had asked for a small reprieve.

"T-Shae, I need a break," he said as Natasha watched Nivea try on her fifth pair of Jordans. "Here's my card. I'll meet you and Nivea in about 20 minutes."

Natasha laughed and took the AMEX from him. Today, they were reaping all the benefits of Antonio's absence from their lives.

"It's fine. I understand. We'll probably be in the dress shop across the hall once she finally decides what she wants," Natasha said.

"Anything for my girls," he said, flashing a smile at Nivea. He winked his eye at Natasha and strolled off.

"Sweetie, just get both pairs," Natasha told Nivea after 10 more minutes of her indecisiveness. "You have to be tired, and I need to find a dress for tonight."

She saw Nivea check the watch on her wrist and perk up.

"Ok, I'll get both," she said quickly and took both shoeboxes to the counter. She'd been grinning furiously she they'd met Antonio outside the mall. He was as happy to see her again as she was to see him.

After Natasha paid for the shoes, they went to find Natasha a dress for Amauri and Paden's party.

"You love my dad, don't you?" Nivea asked as they were leaving the shoe store.

She wanted a family again; it was no secret. Her father being here was all she needed. Natasha looking into the very excited eyes of her daughter and had to admit that she too was glad to have

Antonio back in her life. Somehow, it felt like he never left. They were easy together; it was effortless with him.

"I will always love Antonio," said Natasha, stopping to grab her daughter's hand. "Don't you miss Donte?"

The two hadn't spoken much about him since he'd stormed out of their lives. But Natasha needed her daughter to know that no matter what she did, Nivea's best interests were at the forefront.

"Donte left us," Nivea said with a shrug. "Daddy is here and he wants to be here forever."

Natasha noticed that while her teenager was speaking, she was looking past Natasha, not at her. Natasha turned to find Antonio down on bended knee.

"Natasha, I can't say why our lives have turned out this way, but what I can say is that no other woman in my life has ever made me feel like you do," Antonio began as a crowd formed around them. "Time has only made me secure in this…I'm positive that I don't want another day without you in my life. Be my wife. Please?"

Natasha was speechless. From the look on Nivea's face, it was clear that the two had planned this whole affair. She actually wished she could laugh at the irony of all of it. She'd been proposed to twice in one year. Years ago, she couldn't even get a date. She turned her attention to Antonio again, whose eye revealed a worried look. She desperately wanted to tell him no, that she'd specifically told him this morning that she needed time to process her life. Suddenly, she felt her head shaking yes and heard Antonio scream in elation.

"She said yes!"

He placed the ring on her finger and lifted her in the air. As he swung her around, the crowd cheered in response. Nivea began to cry tears of joy. She was about to get the family she wanted after all this time.

"I love you Mom and Daddy," Nivea said between tears.

Natasha stared at her daughter and now-fiancé with unsure eyes. What had she just done? Hadn't she just asked the Lord to send her a sign about what to do? Was this her sign? She thought about how she and the rest of her First Ladies' Club members talked about how the counterfeit often came before the promise. Was this the promise and was Donte her counterfeit? Either way, Natasha had never felt so confused in her life.

The entire ride home with Nivea, she'd been quiet. The gleaming diamond reminded her that she was about to be someone's wife again. And she couldn't help but feel slightly irritated with her daughter for deceiving her.

"Mom, you look mad. Aren't you happy?" Nivea asked her when they'd reached their home.

"Baby, I am. I'm just overwhelmed," she said, returning a half-smile to her daughter. She didn't want to hurt Nivea, but she also didn't want to lie.

She saw Nivea smile again, her face filled the hope of the future. But if she only knew just how uncertain her mother was about their future. Honestly, she just wanted to call Donte. He always knew what to do after she poured her life out to him. But he hadn't answered any of her calls since she last saw him.

"...And then I had to hurry and get ready to come here," Natasha said to Shenae, falling back into her present moment.

She realized that any future thoughts about the engagement would have to wait; they were here now to celebrate Amauri and Bishop Paden.

"You need a show," Shenae told Natasha and they laughed. "We all do."

"Yes, we do. Look, here's one of our cast members now," said Natasha, pointing toward Lynette.

SHENAE

They called Lynette over to them. She wore an exquisite, lavender floor-length dress with dangling, diamond earrings.

"Girl, I thought my earrings were flashy," Lynette said, noticing Natasha's ring immediately. "Wait. Did you say yes to Donte?"

"No. She said yes to Antonio," Shenae answered for Natasha.

"Nivea's father?" asked a surprised Lynette. "Whoa."

Natasha was beginning to regret leaving her house this morning.

"I didn't really say yes," she reminded Shenae. "I'm going to go find Antonio. I'll see you guys inside."

Lynette looked after Natasha to be nosey and see who her mystery fiancé was. She met a dangerously tall man in the lobby who

Lynette assumed was Antonio. Again, she was glad that someone else's drama was able to shadow her own. She still hadn't really wanted to share what she'd been going through with Pastor Andre and Harriet. She had learned in her walk with God to just keep going. She'd lost count of how many times she'd put a Band-Aid over her pain in an effort to keep up appearances. It wasn't like she didn't want to share her life with her sisters; she just didn't want to bring anyone down. Besides, she'd just enjoyed some intimate time with Pastor Andre before they left for the party. She would relish in that, she thought, winking her eye in her husband's direction.

"I know she still misses Donte," said Shenae to Lynette.

Lynette agreed. Natasha looked happy, but they knew her well enough to realize each time she looked toward the door, she was hoping Donte would walk in.

Meanwhile, guests were arriving left and right and the greenhouse was filled with music and chatter. So many people had turned out to honor the couple. They'd even seen some of the more famous First Ladies in the bunch. One even wore a gaudy church hat with her fancy pantsuit. This, of course, gave Shenae a bittersweet feeling. Not that she missed all the issues and scandals of being a First Lady, but she did miss some of the stylish perks. She'd defied them today and wore a fitted black-and-white dress with mock buttons across the center, red stilettos, a small cornered hat. She looked fierce and she knew it.

"Wow…you look, just wow," she heard a man coming up behind

her.

She turned and saw Angelo, visually drinking in the baddest woman in the room. She was gorgeous. Shenae noted that he looked might dapper in his black blazer paired with a silver shirt and pinstriped tie. His shoulders stood broad and he looked like he'd just stepped out the pages of *GQ*. Shenae nearly swooned. Joining him was another woman who she guess was his sister.

"Hello, Warrior. You look absolutely amazing," Angelo complimented her again with a hug.

"Hello Angelo," Shenae said, unable to voice the butterflies doing gymnastics in her tummy.

The woman beside him was very thin and dressed in a very modest, very tacky robe-dress. Shenae hoped that the poorly dressed woman was hiding a more fly dress underneath the sheet she'd worn.

"Shenae, this sister my sister," introduced Angelo. "Kenya, this is Shenae."

They shook hands pleasantly and Shenae took them over to meet her friends. She could hear the muffled sounds of laughter from the ladies in the group at Kenya's ensemble.

"Sis, we are going to mingle, we'll see you later," Lynette said, grabbing Natasha's arm and scurrying quickly from the circle.

"Shenae, you used to be a First Lady, yes?" inquired Kenya.

Shenae shook her head in response. "Yes, why?"

"I was hoping that my brother has spoken so highly of would be more appropriately dressed," Kenya said, her eyes traveling up and down Shenae's body. "Hhmmm."

Shenae paused. Not only had his sister just cut her with her words but Shenae had also caught Kenya shake her head in disapproval.

"I'm sorry?" Shenae asked, daring her to repeat her insult.

"Uh, Sis, why don't I get you a seat at our table and escort Sheane outside to meet Amauri and Bishop Paden?" Angelo offered, sensing that trouble was brewing.

Shenae scoffed as she watched them walk off. Never in her life had another woman of God boldly disrespected her that way. She'd heard of Kenya's type, covering themselves up head-to-toe because they felt like exposing any type of skin was sinful.

Angelo returned to the lobby to find steam blowing out of Shenae's ears. He shook his head and walked over to her. Angelo had warned his sister not to embarrass him, but she always did. She was a devout Christian woman who believed that the only time skin should be shown was in the bedroom with one's husband. From what his father had shared with him, Kenya hadn't always been that way, but he hadn't shared anything further than that. Somehow Angelo knew that introducing her to Shenae would cause tension considering how closed-minded Kenya was.

When he joined Shenae again, Angelo pulled her in for a hug. This time he lingered in it, absorbing her irritation and giving her his peace. He had to admit Shenae's outfit was sexy, but it didn't offend him. As he held her, she let him slide his hand into the middle of her back. He held her closer to keep her from pulling away. He simply wanted her to realize that he didn't just like her as friend.

"This is nice," Shenae whispered to him, overwhelmed by his intoxicating scent.

Everything that made her a woman began to hum from the strength she felt with him. When Angelo released Shenae, she admitted to herself that fighting against their obvious chemistry was futile. Whatever God was brewing between them was meant to be explored and not stifled. When the embrace was over, their eyes met. Shenae's were filled something he hadn't seen in her yet. It was hope, hope that the two of them would ride this wave out together. Angelo's hand cupped the side of her face. He wished he could kiss her right now in front of everyone and claim her, but he'd wait for the day their relationship became permanent. Instead, he held her hand.

"Hello, Nae."

Shenae swung around in response to the voice that called her.

"Leon?" she exclaimed. "What...what are you doing here?"

She held Angelo's hand firmly now, even though he was trying to pull away. She would not let Leon ruin what she was letting herself feel at that moment. She had nothing to hide.

"I came to see you," she heard the man who'd put her through Hell try to explain.

Leon had grown thinner since Shenae saw him last, but his slick smile remained.

"I left you messages to let you know I was coming home, but they went unreturned," Leon told her. "I heard through the old congregation that you were throwing a party for one of the Daughters and I thought that I should be here to support you. That's what companions do, right? They support each other."

Shenae wanted to laugh at his companion comment. He wasn't the first to insult her with words today. Leon, on the other hand, was serious. He hadn't missed the man standing next to his wife. Whoever he was, he'd be gone soon. Leon had been waiting a long time to see Shenae again and to make amends for what he'd done. If there was another man, so be it; he was up for the challenge.

Shenae took note of both men sizing the other up. Lynette saw the standoff and grabbed her husband and Antonio to intervene. This was neither the time nor the place to start a brawl.

Seeing the two men rushing over, Angelo let go of Shenae's hand and gestured toward them that everything was OK.

"Shenae, why don't I give you a moment to sort this out" Angelo said. "I'll be inside with my sister."

He walked away feeling territorial over Shenae but also very sorry for the former pastor. His wife, whom he hadn't seen in over a year, was holding hands with a man he'd never seen before at a party hosted by an organization that he'd encouraged her to start. Angelo couldn't imagine how he'd feel if that were him fresh out of jail.

As Angelo walked away from her, Leon was walking toward her. Shenae immediately felt the sickening reality that he was about to try to touch her.

"Nae, I'm loving this dress on you," Leon complimented her, sliding his hands up her arms. "It's so good to see you."

He flashed a genuine smile at her and she returned it with a fake one. Shenae knew that, no matter what Leon said, she was ready to move on. She was ready to let go and remove him completely so that she could move on with Angelo. In fact, if she'd known he was coming, she would've brought a fresh pack of divorce papers for him to sign on the spot.

"Shenae, the guests of honor are here," Ny said, running over to her. She shot a puzzled look at Leon, her husband who was supposed to be incarcerated. "Er...are you ready for the entrance?"

Ny gave Leon a smile in an effort to be gracious. Shenae looked pleased to escape the moment and followed Ny to the front entranceway so they could welcome the couple walking in.

AMAURI

As Bishop Paden and his wife approached the entrance, the couple was taken aback by the extravagance of it all. The lights from the greenhouse danced under the moonlight and upon entering the lobby of the great room, they were greeted with cheers and applause from their closest friends.

Amauri wore a yellow one-shoulder, floor-length gown with her hair swept up into a bun. Bishop Paden's tailored tuxedo screamed opulence, his shirt the same color as his wife's dress. The two looked like a couple drawn together.

Upon entering the greenhouse, where their other friends and church members were located, the lead band member announced the couple's arrival, and everyone stopped to cheer. Bishop Paden laughed heartily, touched by the outpour of love in the building. It almost felt like they were reliving their wedding reception 10 years ago.

Amauri searched the crowd and found familiar faces with genuine smiles on their faces. It warmed her heart to know both she and her husband were loved this much. She felt the tears overwhelm her as she noticed a very familiar face in the crowd—Mason, her grandmother Meemaw's best friend. Amauri released her husband and ran into his arms.

"Mason how are you? It's so good to see you," Amauri said, trying not to ruin her makeup.

Years ago, her Meemaw and Mason secretly loved each other. But growing up in an era of hideous racism, neither could admit to the interracial love they shared. It had been Mason who encouraged Amauri to follow her heart, even when her own mother had so fiercely rejected Paden.

"I wanted to surprise you," Mason said.

He was always so soft spoken and humble. His eyes danced with joy as he saw her standing there. He couldn't help himself from the elation he felt that she was coming back to New York to live closer to him. He hoped that it meant she would mend her broken relationship with her mother.

"Please, come and let me introduce you to my friends," Amauri said, joining hands with him and going to find her fellow Daughters.

Bishop Paden, now left to mingle alone, smiled as he saw his wife's grandmother's friendhad come to support Amauri. He hated that the love between Meemaw and Mason wasn't embraced because of their strict families. It was a reality that he had grown to understand. Some people could never grasp that love was colorblind, and he was determined to raise children that treated everyone with the same respect, love, and dignity they wanted to receive.

He wasn't foolish, though. He knew some of the world didn't like to see him and Amauri together. They'd dealt with more prejudice than a little bit. He applauded himself for the things that he'd overcome from his past, but some nights it troubled him. He'd shaken himself out of nightmares many nights remembering the things he'd done and seen in the streets of New York. He had never told Amauri the full truth, because he wasn't ready to face that demon yet.

"Pade? Is that you?" Kenya said, reaching to grab Paden's arm.

It had been over 14 years since she'd seen him. He was her first love, and even after all these years, she still hadn't extinguished him from her system. He looked the part of a pastor now, all distinguished and prominent—a far cry from the Paden she knew. She never imagined that she would ever see him again after the horrifying beating she'd witnessed him receive in New York. The gang he'd tried to leave had left him to die in the middle of an alley, blood seeping from every crevice it seemed. The night before the beating, Paden had told Kenya that he felt like something was calling him. He wasn't sure what it was but he couldn't be a gang member anymore. Kenya remembered begging him to stay; she didn't have anyone else. As her father's bastard child, she'd been shunned from his family and had run away from her whore of a mother's house. She had lived a hard life by the time she met Paden, full of mistakes and regrets. She knew that once Paden was gone, there would be no one to protect her anymore. And she was right; she'd been tossed out like trash once he was gone for good.

"K, what are you doing here?" Paden found himself looking straight into the eyes of his first love.

He'd loved her since they were in middle school. He'd protected her from all her bad mistakes and then tried his hardest to claim her as his own when they were older. Now, more than anything, Kenya was the past that he wanted to keep buried. He looked around, trying to spot his wife. He didn't want Amauri to find him and start asking questions, questions that would unearth his past.

"Is that all you have to say to me after all these years?" Kenya asked, taking offense. "All this time has passed and all you can say to me is 'What are you doing here?' I had no idea that you would be here, *Bishop Paden*."

She emphasized his new title as a warning. He owed her an explanation for his new identity.

"I'm sorry, K," he said, trying to calm her. "It's just been a long time."

He attempted to get closer to her before she caused a scene. Kenya, thinking he was trying to hug her, threw her hand to stop him from moving toward her. She held back her tears, determined not to let him hold her. Glancing over at his wife in the yellow dress, she felt the pangs of jealousy. Kenya had loved Paden Raleigh for over 20 years, but she was the woman he'd chosen. She watched Amauri laugh and smile and entertain her guests with another black, elderly man on her arm. It drove the dagger further into her heart.

"I see you are doing well with your little snowflake over there," she said, her voice filled with icy contempt.

"My wife's name is Amauri," Bishop Paden firmly corrected her.

He saw Angelo coming toward them.

"Hey man, glad you could make it," Paden extended his hand to Angelo.

"Thanks for inviting me. Great party," Angelo responded, standing by Kenya's side. "I see you've met my sister Kenya. Kenya, this is the guy whose car broke down and I helped him get to where he was going. Do you remember?"

"Yes. I remember very well," Kenya responded, her eyes not moving from Paden's face.

Bishop Paden's eyes hadn't moved from Kenya's either. Kenya gave him the iciest smile she could.

"Paden, sweetie!" they all heard Amauri call as she joined them. "Let's dance!"

Out on the dance floor, Natasha and Antonio had paired up, along

First Ladies Club: Rocks, Rings and Resurrections

with Lynette and Andre who were also enjoying the music.

"Hello Angelo," Amauri said, spotting him next to the woman in the hideous frock.

"Amauri," greeted Angelo, giving her a hug. "You look divine tonight. This is my sister, Kenya."

It was another dagger in Kenya's heart.

"Nice to meet you," said Amauri to Kenya. "I'm Amauri, and I love your brother. Especially the way he has my sister, Shenae, smiling."

"Pleased to meet you, First Lady," Kenya said, refusing to touch the bubbly Amauri's hand.

Everyone in the circle seemed to notice the awkwardness, but Amauri didn't let it phase her.

"Well, I'm glad you could come," she responded. "Now, excuse me as I steal my husband for a dance. We are so happy to have such a great group of friends."

She noticed a shift in her husband's demeanor since he'd held her hand last. He seemed angry now. As they danced together, he seemed to be in a faraway place, constantly looking past her and not paying much attention to what she was saying. She was honestly glad when the song was over and it was announced that dinner would be served in the next room. Amauri wanted to know what was bothering her husband on such a special night.

"So, Natasha, do you want to tell us about that rock on your hand?" Lynette said, once they'd all sat down to eat.

At the table were all the Deborah's Daughters and their plus-ones, Kenya, Mason, and two empty chairs.

Natasha could feel the heat rising in her cheeks as she stuffed a piece of bread in her mouth to prevent her from responding.

"Come on now," Amauri said, unaware that Natasha had gotten engaged earlier that day. "Let us see it."

Natasha held her hand out toward the middle of the table, receiving gasps and sounds of appreciation from the ladies at the table.

"Girl, that is awesome," said Amauri, a little confused that Donte wasn't with her. "You finally told Donte yes!"

"Actually she didn't. That's not my ring," said Donte, taking the empty seat at the table.

All eyes were on him at that moment. They'd never seen him so dressed up. For Donte, it was either his Armor Bearer suit or those ridiculous Hawaiian shirts he wore sometimes. Tonight, adorned in an all-white tux with a black bowtie, he was the picture of sexiness. Natasha grabbed her stomach, as she suddenly felt lovesick.

"Don—Donte," she stammered, forcing the rising butterflies back down into their cage.

"Hello Natasha, nice ring," he told her. "Congrats to you both."

He congratulated Antonio with his free hand; on his other arm was Melissa, the woman that had done everything in her power to gain Donte's affection in the past year. Of course, he hadn't wanted to come alone, but Natasha hated that he'd brought her, of all people. She shot a fake smile in Natasha's direction as she and Donte took their seats. Melissa was clutching his arm as if he was an anchor. She wanted to say something, but the words escaped her. Maybe it was the tux he was wearing or the newfound charisma he was carrying. Either way, Natasha felt further from Donte than she had in a long time.

"I'm so glad to be here and to be apart of your night, Bishop Paden. I'm sad to see you go, but I'm happy for all that God is doing in your life," Donte said to the couple.

"I'm so glad that God has connected us all," Paden responded, avoiding Kenya's gaze in his direction. "We are blessed to be a part of this family that has both changed and helped us in so many ways."

"This night just makes me so happy. I'd like to propose a toast if that's ok," Amauri said, calling the waiters over with the glasses of champagne.

They'd allowed champagne at the party for the toasts and nothing else. Everyone at the table took a glass. A photographer from a popular magazine stood by to capture the moment.

Amauri stood at that moment and Paden moved to join her. A familiar pain overcame him as he tried to stand. His knee had given him problems for over a decade now, all stemming from when he'd been jumped in New York. His former gang members had only given him one way to officially leave them; he had to be jumped out just as he'd been jumped in when he joined. He remembered them, his so-called brothers, pounding on him until he was black and blue. He'd spent nights in Kenya's apartment, afraid that if he went home, they'd find him and bring more punishment. Now, it had crept up on him as he'd been skipping out on workouts lately with so much going on. He cringed and clutched the table for support.

"Oh my goodness, Paden," said Amauri, clutching his arm to support him. "Are you ok?"

It was the most inopportune time, but Paden found himself looking at Kenya. She carried a worried expression on her face. The rest of the circle looked at him, obviously in pain.

"Oh, I'm fine. Don't fuss over this old man's knees," Bishop Paden said smoothly, collecting himself. The crowd laughed and prepared for the toast. They all raised their glasses after Amauri delivered an eloquent speech about love, life, and everlasting friendship.

"Cheers!" they all exclaimed and the couple sat down.

Bishop Paden took care this time to shift his weight to the other side as he took his seat.

"That knee still bothering you, Pade?" Kenya asked him from across the table.

She remembered many nights, sitting up with him as she nursed his knee. It had been her that had bandaged and cleaned him up after he was bludgeoned nearly to death. It wasn't something that he could go to the hospital for, so he'd stayed with her, the woman who loved him.

"Wait. How do you know about his knee?" Amauri questioned her.

Paden had described a horrific car accident that he miraculously walked away from years ago. All that remained, he said, was a little knee pain and some bad memories. How could Kenya know about any of that? And who was Pade? Amauri turned from Kenya to her husband. Neither said a word.

"BP, is there something we need to talk about?" Amauri asked him in a low voice.

She'd gotten everyone's attention just now with her comment to Kenya. Each one was waiting for the explanation of how Bishop Paden knew the woman in the robe-dress.

"Sweetheart, we can discuss this later," he said in her ear. "Let's enjoy the night."

He kissed her on her cheek just as the servers came to bring the main course to the table. Amauri could feel the air leaving her; she'd never been more embarrassed in her life. Her friends seemed to have let the moment pass, but all Amauri wanted to do was scream at Paden for what he was obviously trying to keep from her.

After dessert was served, most of the guests moved back to the greenhouse to dance again. Lynette wanted to take a keepsake photo with all the members of Deborah's Daughters, so they all scurried to find the perfect backdrop.

Bishop Paden knew that he needed to explain to Kenya why he left her all those years ago. The fact that she remembered the pain in his knee meant that she still cared for him. He wouldn't lie that some old feelings resurfaced when he'd seen her. She used to be so young and vibrant and beautiful. Now, she just looked like life had caught up to her, like the weight of the world had fallen on her. It was Paden's only explanation for the fact that she was now hiding herself behind that drape. He saw her sitting at the table alone. She looked as sad as she had when he'd walked away from her years ago.

"Hey kid," Paden tried using the affectionate term they shared.

"Don't 'kid' me, Pade. I don't want to be here any longer," Kenya responded, her eyes still filled with pain.

"I've been preaching," he began to explain. "That night Pastor Gaither found me in front of his brownstone. He and his wife took me in. They connected me with my spiritual parents here in Atlanta to get cleaned up."

He took a seat beside her and tried to get her to look at him.

"It was God calling me all that time ago, Kenya. I'm sorry that I couldn't take you with me, but I had to get clean by myself before I could help anyone else," Paden said.

He sighed. It was the first time in a long time that he was just being a man. He was in front of her now, without the collar and without the title. He knew that what he did hurt Kenya, and he wanted her to know that he felt remorse for the effect of his actions on her life.

"I know you couldn't come back for me, Paden. I had my own demons back then," said Kenya, fidgeting with the bracelet on her wrist. "I heard you married a white girl, but I never thought...after knowing the Paden I knew, that it would last."

She looked behind her and saw Amauri searching the greenhouse, probably looking for Paden.

"She doesn't know anything, does she?" Kenya asked him quietly.

Paden shook his head in defeat. He knew, after tonight, he'd have to come clean to his wife soon or later. He loved Amauri.

"What does she know, Paden?" Kenya pressed. "What all haven't you told her?"

"Kenya, look. I don't want to talk about that. I don't feel like it's any of your business."

The words stung Kenya where she sat.

"My business?!" she hissed. "Do you even know what they did to me when you abandoned me? They—."

She felt tears of anger welling in her ducts.

"I'm glad the grass was greener on the other side for you," Kenya spew at him. "Green and clean...and white."

It didn't make much sense, but Kenya just wanted to hurt him. He was forcing her to relive the roughest time in her life by sitting in front of her now all high and mighty.

"That's out of line, Kenya. I never meant to hurt you. You meant everything to me. I had to go with God."

"So you're telling that when you found God that you couldn't come and find me?" she asked him, the intensity in her voice growing. "You couldn't have come back and told me about Jesus? No. I had to find Him the hard way...all by myself."

"My life had moved on," Paden said. "I never stopped praying for you. I never stopped asking God to send someone to help you escape. I had to get out of that life."

His words were simple and heartfelt, but he knew that in Kenya was a secret that could shatter his life. Bishop Paden reached out and placed his hand onto hers. It was a gesture meant to calm and comfort her; he could see the tears in her eyes.

Watching from afar, Amauri saw him touch her and realized she couldn't take it anymore. She wouldn't wait to find out what was going on between the two of them. She picked up the skirt of her dress and marched over toward them.

"Look, I hear you, Paden," responded Kenya to Paden's comforting touch. "I wish I could forgive you for leaving me, but I can't."

She snatched her hand from his just as Amauri reached them.

"Hey sweetie," said Amari, standing over them like a teacher who had caught two schoolmates talking during a test.

She looked like a woman ready to go to war, and after all she had endured by this man's side over the years, she would. No devil would steal what God had built between them. She saw her husband offer the seat on the other side of him and exhale out loud before he began to speak.

"Kenya and I were in a relationship about 14 years ago, before I went to Wesleyn College and met you," he said to Amauri. "I haven't seen her since then, and I didn't know she'd be here today. I had no clue she was Angelo's sister."

"Oh," Amauri said, taking some time to process what she'd just heard. She'd been ready for everything, she thought, but not a woman from BP's past that she'd never been privy to. This meant that this woman knew the Paden she didn't know. He only gave her bits and pieces of his life before her, citing that it was too painful to discuss. Had he meant that leaving Kenya was painful? She found herself drowning in her thoughts.

"Babe?" Paden tried to get her attention again.

"Um, ok...well, I'm glad that you could reconnect after all these years," Amauri said, quickly standing. "Is there something else you'll be needed from my husband, Kenya?"

She held her hand out for her husband to join her away from the table.

"I don't need anything else from your husband ever again," remarked Kenya. "You can surely take him."

Amauri hadn't missed Kenya's dig in that statement, but she wouldn't allow this women to make her lose herself. God have given her more than she'd ever dreamed was possible, and it wouldn't be ruined by the bite of a bitter ex.

"Great, have a nice evening," Amauri responded, hooking her arm in Paden's and returning to the greenhouse.

Angelo walked over to sit with Kenya, oblivious to the drama that had just unfolded at the table. His eyes were fixed on Shenae, who'd been sitting at another table in uncomfortable conversation with her husband. He'd been keeping an eye on them from the lobby, just in case Shenae needed him to intervene. She would occasionally look over in his direction to assure him that she was ok.

"That's her ex-husband, isn't it?" Kenya asked her brother.

He nodded in response, still keeping watch over the two. Kenya wanted to warn him not to trust the feelings he was having. Love was an awful emotion; it held you captive and never let go.

"Angelo, she has to handle this herself," he heard Kenya say. "People have to live with their own choices."

It was something she knew firsthand.

"I'm fine," he responded. "I know she has to be the one that breaks that tie."

He decided then that he wouldn't intervene after all. This was her battle to fight.

"Besides, you know," he commented out loud. "We're just getting to know each other, so I'm good."

NATASHA

"Is my fiancée enjoying herself?" Antonio asked.

The two were slow dancing together amongst the other guests.

"Yes, I am," she responded.

"That ring looks nice on you," he said, grabbing her hand and kissing it.

She tried not to cringe in response.

"Antonio, I need some water. Will you excuse me?"

He nodded and she hurried off the dance floor to find something to drink. She opened the doors of the greenhouse to get some fresh air in the outside garden.

Antonio watched her as she disappeared outside. He knew that the road back to her heart wouldn't be easy, but more than anything, he wanted to make it work. He knew she was unsure about their future, but she'd said yes to him. And for now, that was all he needed—a chance.

Outside, Natasha took a seat on the stone bench among the flowers.

"So when did you get the ring?" she heard a voice join her outside.

It was Donte, standing before her again in all white. Natasha had to swallow hard before she answered. She definitely didn't want to disclose the details of the engagement, or whatever she was calling it, to him.

"Today," Natasha said. "When did you take interest in Melissa?"

He laughed, wondering why she would ask him something like that.

"God can bring people together after the craziest of circumstances, right?" he asked her. "You should know that."

Natasha wanted to respond, she wanted to ask Donte if he was talking about him and Melissa or him and her. Unable to find the words, she just looked at him looking at her.

Donte stood looking into Natasha's eyes, wishing he could say all that was on his heart. He knew it made Natasha sick to see him with Melissa. He was just as sick to see her with Antonio.

"Natash—," Donte began, but was interrupted by Melissa who had joined them.

"There you are," Melissa said, hanging on his arm again. "I was thinking we could go back to my place and...oh, hello there, Natasha. Didn't see you."

Melissa giggled. Natasha wanted to gag but turned her head away instead.

"Donte and I were having a conversation," Natasha reminded her of what she'd just interrupted.

"Oh, sweetie," Melissa said to Donte. "I thought we were leaving soon."

"Yeah, you're right," he responded to Melissa. "I think I saw Bishop Paden leaving the building, so I guess there's no reason for us to stick around. Have a good night, Natasha."

Donte turned and left Natasha there with her thoughts. She looked up to see Melissa glance back and flash her a sly smile. There was nothing worse than a woman like Melissa, Natasha thought. She had thrown herself at Donte for months, and now it looked as if he was falling for it. She thought he was smarter than that, but maybe he was going along with it to embarrass her. People did strange things when they were hurt. Natasha decided that it was better to forgive him now than to hold a grudge.

Antonio watched Natasha from the greenhouse, trying to give her as much space as he could. He wasn't crazy enough to think that Natasha and Donte would just end overnight. But he was willing to wait for as long as he needed to finally have Natasha to himself. She was the only woman he could see himself spending the rest of his life with.

"Hey beautiful, are you ready to go?" Antonio asked, putting his jacket around her.

She stood up and he pulled her into his arms. Natasha could feel his warmth taking over her. He felt so good, but she had to remain strong. She'd keep her virtue at all cost, even if she was a little sad that Donte had walked away from her again.

"I'm actually going to leave with Shenae," she told him, releasing his arms from her waist. "I'll call you in the morning."

He leaned down and she met him halfway for a soft kiss. He was disappointed. He thought that they'd be spending the night together.

"Are you sure? I was thinking that we could go back to my hotel and watch a movie or something."

His smile told her the movie was not all he wanted to share that night. She could read right through him.

"I'm sure," she said. "Good night. I'll see you in the morning before service."

He kissed her again and walked away.

SHENAE

"Not going home with your new hubby?" Shenae asked, joining her friend's side.

Natasha laughed.

"Girl, you look beat but still beautiful," she said, pushing a strand of Shenae's hair out of her face.

That unruly strand had been more annoying to Shenae tonight than Leon had.

"Thanks sis. I'd say we put on a real party," Shenae said, seeing Angelo hugging his sister goodbye.

Natasha caught her smiling when he started walking toward them.

"Girl, you have it bad," she teased Shenae. "I don't want to be the third wheel. Let me go and see if I can get another ride home."

"No, wait with me," Shenae said, holding Natasha back.

She knew that she shouldn't get too excited because she'd not seen Leon for the last hour. He was probably waiting for her outside. She'd done all she could to dodge him, but he'd cornered her at least three times over the course of the evening.

"So, Beautiful Warrior, are you almost ready to go?" Angelo asked her, kissing her cheek. "I was thinking that I could take you home. What do you think?"

"Only if Natasha is ok with driving my car home," Shenae said, nudging her. "I'll just get it from you tomorrow at church."

"Oh, so you're assuming that I'll just come get you in the morning?" Angelo was flirting with her.

Shenae blushed. She was new to flirting and wasn't hip to the banter between two people developing feelings. She was trying to keep up with the charming Angelo but often found herself resorting to a shy giggle.

"I'm kidding. I'd love to come get you for church in the morning," he said to Shenae.

She giggled again and gave Natasha her car keys. She saw her friend shake her head in disbelief. Shenae knew she acted like a silly girl around Angelo but she couldn't help it.

"I'll see you in the morning," Natasha said, kissing her cheek. "Good night, Angelo."

Natasha went to find Lynette to say farewell before she called it a night.

"So where is he?" Angelo asked, looking around the corner for Leon. "Should I be afraid to hug you right now?"

"He's gone I think," responded Shenae, grabbing his hand and heading toward the building. "I won't tell you that it's completely over in his mind though. He is very adamant about seeing me now that he's out of jail."

He held open the front entrance door for her and they roamed through the parking lot together.

"I'm okay with him seeing you again," he finally told her. "I understand that you have some business you need to handle, but it's been almost a year. He has to know that you would move on eventually, right?"

"I guess," Shenae said, thinking about it. "I guess we both thought we'd never be divorced, you know? I've loved my husband from the first time I saw him. We've raised two children and started a church together. We have a history."

Shenae knew that there was no excuse for what her husband did, but she was willing to forgive Leon now that she'd come out on top of this whole mess. Seeing her soon-to-be-ex-husband tonight made her realize that she did still care about him; she was glad to know that he was trying to get back on his feet.

"It's just complicated, you know," she finished as they reached

Angelo's car.

"I can't say that I do," he responded. "My wife decided that rather than work out our issues, she'd find an outside comfort. She misled me for a long time and, in the end, dragged my children through the mud."

He remembered how much pain their mother's mess had caused the whole family. In the end, Angelo wished he could've bore the burden of their pain along with his own.

"I can't say I just forgave her because it was my Christian duty," he continued. "People should be held responsible for their actions and accept the consequences. Even if those consequences mean divorce."

"Wait," said Shenae, sensing she'd struck a nerve. "I never said that he shouldn't be held responsible for his actions."

"No, but you found it necessary to walk me down your memory lane of love," Angelo said, letting her hand go. "This man deceived you and his whole congregation. You see him today for the first time and just let him back in that easy? Really, Shenae?"

He hadn't meant to sound so harsh, but he'd just seen how affected she was by her ex and it bothered him. Shenae had neglected him, her date, the whole night. She'd said she wanted to be more than just friends, and he refused to extend himself to another woman and have her betray him.

"Angelo, wait. What's wrong? I never meant to hurt your feelings.

I was just—."

"No, it's cool," he said, rubbing a hand through his slicked back hair. "Listen. I'm going to call it a night. I'll just talk to you later."

He hopped into his car, leaving Shenae in the parking lot with a growing sadness in her eyes. She watched him pull out of the parking spot and zoom past her. She had no idea what just happened. Shenae picked up the phone to call him and decided against it, realizing that maybe she'd gone too far. One minute the two were talking about him taking her home and the next, they were talking about her ex. She chastised herself for sharing so much about Leon at that moment. It wasn't like she could take it back now; he was already gone.

Shenae ran to her own car to find Natasha in the driver's seat. She opened the passenger's side door and slumped into the seat, startling Natasha.

"Oh no," said Natasha, grabbing her arm. "What happened?"

"I don't want to talk about it," said Shenae. "Let's just get home."

"I'm ok with that," Natasha said, starting the car.

After dropping Natasha off at home, Shenae tried Angelo's phone. He sent her straight to voicemail, of course. Pulling into her own driveway, she sat for a few minutes in the car. Shenae hoped to God that she hadn't ruined a good thing before it was able to take off.

First Ladies Club: Rocks, Rings and Resurrections

What a day, she thought to herself, opening her glove compartment to pull out the marquee diamond that Leon had placed on her finger when they exchanged vows. She stared at it for a long time and felt the memories of what the ring once meant. It was a symbol of love and devotion, and she'd believed back then that God was at the core of their circle of love. In fact, Shenae had to admit that when she was telling Angelo all those things about Leon, she had felt something. It wasn't all gone; they had a history. And it was a complicated history like she had said. He was once a great man and an amazing husband. She decided she would call Leon tomorrow and maybe they could have coffee.

She dragged herself into the condo and opened the door to complete silence. How lonely, she sighed to herself. Shenae couldn't believe that, after all this time, she actually felt lonely again. She showered and put on her satin pajamas. She had decided to call it a night when her phone rang.

"Hello?" she answered.

"Hello," the voice said. "Can you come to the door? I'm here."

"Um, ok?" she said, walking to her front door.

Shenae took a few minutes to groom in the mirror on the wall in front of the door. She removed the satin scarf from her hair and let the strands fall free. She then made sure her pajama top was buttoned all the way. She wanted to make sure she was covered.

She opened the door to find her ex-husband on the other side.

"Hello. I didn't mean to wake you," he said, smiling.

"It's ok, Leon. You didn't. Come in."

She slid to the side so that he could pass. The door was barely closed before he backed her against the tiny wall she had just checked herself out in and seared her with his lips.

AMAURI

Amauri and her husband sat in the limo in silence. She had a feeling that Kenya was only the first tear in the unraveling seam of Paden's past. She was afraid to ask him anymore questions, so afraid that she'd been lied to for 10 years of her life.

As soon as the limo pulled into the driveway of their house, Amauri didn't wait for the driver to come around and let her out. She stormed out of the vehicle and up the stairs to their front door.

"Amauri, let's talk about this," Paden said, running behind her.

He was so disappointed in himself for keeping so much from Amauri. It wasn't even secrets that he'd kept from her out of malice; he simply wanted to keep her safe. If the things of his past came to light, he'd probably end up behind bars like his brother, ripping their family apart. To clear his guilty conscience, Paden had been working with the police for years to help to gang members find rehabilitation in jail. And he'd successfully helped over 50 men get out of gangs using his insight of the system and network.

How could he tell Amauri about all of the pain he'd brought upon so many families? Bishop Paden was deeply indebted to God for forgiving him and teaching him how to use what he knew to help men and women get free from the lifestyle he'd escaped successfully. He knew his wife wasn't ready to handle that. There were life choices that he'd made that he was determined to keep secret. Knowing them would ultimately hurt his wife, and he knew she'd leave him. Paden loved his family more than anything, and every sacrifice he'd made was to keep them safe from harm.

"Amauri!"

She'd reached the top of the stairs by the time he'd even made his way into the house.

"I have nothing to say, Paden," she appeared at the top of the flight. "Oh, I'm sorry. It's 'Pade,' right?"

She looked down on him like he was the scum of the earth. She was actually more embarrassed than mad at him, but it was enough to make her look at him in a different light.

"Look, come down here so we can talk about this," Paden pleaded. "The kids are asleep, and we need to talk."

"No," she screamed at him, the pain in her voice shining through.

"Amauri Raleigh, I know you are angry, but I need you to get down here so we can talk," Paden said.

"Are you ordering me?" Amauri asked in disbelief. "No. I'm going to bed."

"Ugh! You drive me crazy sometimes. Stop being so stubborn. God help me."

Paden's voice rang through the halls, waking one of the babies. They both heard cries coming from the end of the hallway. She'd never heard her husband so angry before.

"Is everything ok?" she heard her nanny, Frieda, open the door to her children's room.

"Yes, Frieda. Everything's fine," Amauri told her. "Just please make sure the babies go back to bed. Bishop Paden and I will be going out for a few hours. We'll see you in the morning."

She walked down the stairs to their living room, searching for her husband in the dark. Amauri found him sitting on the couch, his jacket hanging on one knee. He looked to be deep in thought. She quickly slipped on her running shoes and returned to find him still there, silent as ever.

"C'mon, Paden," Amauri said, reaching for her husband's hands. "Let's take a walk."

He placed his jacket around her shoulders as they stepped outside into their backyard. The grounds surrounding their home were superb. In choosing a home, the two had made sure that greenery surrounded them. Should they ever feel the need to escape, they wanted to make sure they could always find solace in their own backyard. Paden held her hand tight as they walked the outside trail.

"What does Kenya mean to you?" his wife finally asked, her blue eyes as gentle as she could muster.

"She was my first everything," he admitted to her. "I fell in love with her when we were kids, you know? And then, when I left my old life behind, I left her too."

He stopped walking. Amauri could see that he'd become sad. She squeezed his hand a little tighter, hoping it would assure him and he'd continue.

"I heard that…that they'd hurt her when I left," Paden said, tears forming in his eyes. "I was supposed to protect her, Amauri. I hate what they did to her because of me. God, I'm so sorry."

Her husband was crying now, crying hard as he spoke of Kenya. Amauri's jealousy faded as she now understood that what he felt for her was guilt. Seeing Paden, her pillar of strength, crying like this reminded her that he was still a man. He was human, with his own set of insecurities and struggles that had nothing to do with the church.

"Why didn't you tell me about her, Paden?" asked Amauri. "Didn't I deserve to know?"

"Of course you did," he said as she cupped his face and wiped his tears away. "I just didn't know how to talk about her. She is so far in my past that I try not to think about her."

"Is she what's been keeping you awake lately?" his wife asked, probing further. "Is she why you were upset that I went to New York last year?"

Amauri was trying to connect the dots on her own, but she was failing. She needed her husband to tell her what she wanted to know.

"Yes and no. There are things that I can't tell you, because I'm afraid it will put you in danger."

"More secrets? I don't like secrets," Amauri said, walking away from him and into the moonlight. Secrets brought unspeakable pain, she wanted to tell him. They made you doubt the husband you swore you knew.

"Babe, I love you," Bishop Paden said, hugging her from behind. "And I need you to know that I would never hurt you. I'd never hurt our girls."

He planted a kiss on her neck and breathed in her scent.

"I need you. Don't shut me out," he pleaded.

Paden couldn't afford to lose her right now when he was about to confront his greatest fear. New York was more than the start of a new ministry; it was where God delivered him. God had taken him out, and now, for some reason, He was commanding he go back and possibly be found by the same people he ran from years ago.

"I am not going anywhere, Paden," she said, turning to face him. "But you've got to stop keeping things from me. Omitting truth is as bad as distorting it."

He looked at her, his sweet Amauri, begging him to come clean about everything. He remained silent, hoping his last confession about Kenya would be enough for the night.

He saw her sigh. "Walk with me," she said, pulling him further into the trail.

Amauri knew that her husband was still very raw from the vulnerable moment they had just shared. The tall oak trees sheltered them, but the path provided by the moonlight allowed them to walk almost to the edge of their property without getting lost.

"I'd say right is here is perfect," Amauri announced looking around.

"Perfect for what, sweetheart?" Paden questioned. He was emotionally and physically spent. He wanted nothing more than to join his wife in bed and enjoy the comforts of her love.

"For you to make love to me," she answered him, pulling a bag from behind a tree and unveiling its contents. "I had Frieda put this out here for us to enjoy after the party."

He helped her roll out a blanket and she unpacked strawberries for the two of them. The couple laid there on the ground, cuddled together under the moon. Paden looked at his wife and thanked God that He'd chosen her for him. He loved to kiss her, and tonight would be no different.

NATASHA

Natasha wasn't sure how long she'd been bewitched by her left hand. She'd showered the night before looking at it, changed into her pajamas still looking at it, and then she'd gotten into bed and just stared at the diamond ring now on her finger. She'd given up on getting a good night's rest once she remembered how Donte had so easily disregarded her.

"When did he start dressing like that?" she asked herself out loud.

She looked at her ring again and began to pout.

"Mom, are you sleep?" Nivea called from the other side of her mother's closed door.

"No baby, I'm still up. Come in."

Nivea opened the door and ran to jump on her mother's bed. She'd re-braided her hair into cornrows and thrown on the

Atlanta Hawks pajamas Natasha got her two Christmases ago. Natasha remembered that Shawn had thought the pajamas were too boyish, but she knew that her daughter would love them.

"How was the party?" she asked her mother.

"It was good. Are you ready for church in the morning?"

"Of course," Nivea responded, moving to lie on her stomach.

She crossed her legs behind her and thought about her next question before continuing.

"Mom, are you even happy about Dad's proposal?"

Natasha looked at her daughter. Her eyes were as inquisitive now as they were when she was just a child. She wanted to tell her daughter the absolute truth, but she feared that it would be too hard for her teenage mind to understand. Natasha had forgiven Antonio as much as she could in this short amount of time. But, could they really move on? Could they really be the family Natasha imagined 18 years ago?

"Nivea, I'm so glad to have Antonio in our lives again after so much time. I'm happy to see you so happy, and I'm so ready to see you have your father."

She stuttered a little in her response; she'd never been able to lie to her daughter.

"That's not answering the question," Nivea said to her mother. "You two seem to have fallen right back into whatever you had all that time ago, right? But why aren't you jumping for joy or telling everyone?"

"I didn't do that when Donte asked to marry me."

"I know, I know," Nivea said. "I don't know. I guess I just expected something different is all."

"Baby, life is complicated," Natasha informed her daughter. "And if you are happy, then I am too."

"Really, mommy? You're happy?"

"I am so happy," Natasha said, smiling. "Now, let's go to sleep. We have church in the morning."

She pulled back the covers to let her daughter slide in with her. Tonight, she'd relish in Nivea's company. Soon, Nivea was sound asleep, leaving Natasha to stare at her hand again.

Her phone buzzed beside her bed. It was probably Antonio, she thought. She'd forgotten to call him and let him know she'd made it home safely. She put in her earpiece and pressed her thumb and forefinger together on the string to answer.

"Hey, I'm sorry. I'm home," Natasha whispered into the phone, not wanting to wake her sleeping baby.

"You looked amazing tonight, Natasha...I need you to know that I love you."

"Donte?"

Natasha clutched her chest before answering him again.

"Um, hey. Sorry, I wasn't expecting to hear from you," she started. "I...I um..."

She wanted to say it back to him, but couldn't seem to find the courage.

"I know. This is the worst," she heard him say through the phone. "I guess I know now that what we want in life is not always what God desires."

"You don't really mean that, do you?" she asked him, tearing up.

"Look, Natasha. I'm leaving after church tomorrow, and...well, I needed you to know that I loved you before I was gone."

"Leaving?" she exclaimed in horror. "Wait, Donte. Where are you going?"

"I'm going to the mountains for a few weeks. I need to clear my head. I need to hear from God," he told her. "I wish you so much happiness. I need you to hear me say it, because when I come back, it will be to move. I'm moving away from you, but I know that wherever I am, I'll still be hopelessly in love with you."

Natasha tried to stop her tears from falling. She couldn't keep doing this to herself, she thought. She loved this man too much to punish herself because of what other people thought.

"God has me though," Donte assured her. "I promise I'm good."

"Donte, don't go," Natasha begged him.

"I have to, Natasha." he told her. "Goodbye."

The next sound she heard was silence. He'd hung up on her.

"But I love you too," Natasha whispered to an empty earpiece.

She put her head in her hands and cried silently. She cried for the fear she had inside that was keeping her from being truly happy.

"Mommy," Nivea said, turning over.

Natasha could see her daughter's cheeks were wet with tears.

"I heard you. How could you keep yourself from that kind of love?"

"I don't know sweetie," she said, hugging her daughter.

"Well fix it," Nivea urged, crying again. "If you love Donte, then be with him."

Natasha laughed at how brave her daughter wanted her to be.

"Ok, sweetie," she promised. "We'll fix it in the morning."

She would get her man back and get her life in order. Tomorrow would be the best day of her life. Nothing in the world would keep her from it.

SHENAE

Shenae woke up feeling like she'd been hit by a train. She rubbed her temples with both hands as she rose from her sofa. She vaguely remembered the details from the night before—Angelo getting mad at her and storming off. She hoped that she'd dreamed it all up.

"Good morning beautiful," said Leon, smiling.

He was actually smiling a little too hard for Shenae's liking. He was also a little too close to her on the couch.

"Leon, why are you still here?" she asked him, looking at the clock on her wall.

"Girl, after what we shared last night, don't you feel anything?" he asked with the same creepy smile on his face.

"After what we shared?" she laughed at him. "Leon, you kissed me, and I slapped you in the face. And since you were drunk, I couldn't actually kick you out."

She guessed she'd fallen sleep next to him while they watched the movie. This cheap couch was certainly not as comfortable as her bed. She'd be sure to splurge on a new one with her reinstated assets.

"When did you take your shirt off?" she asked, noticing the patch of matted hair on his chest.

Shenae was disgusted with the thought that he may have touched her in her sleep. It had been a long time since she'd been touched by a man. And before that, Leon had been her only lover for 20 years. Shenae felt nausea creep up on her at the smell of the lingering alcohol that was coming from her ex-husband.

"You know what, don't answer that," she decided. "I'm going to take a shower. I have church this morning. Please be gone when I get out. Good day."

With that, she purposely sauntered away from him. She wouldn't hide the gorgeous body that he was never going to touch again. Walking upstairs to her room, she almost gave a shout of praise. It was so good to know that the feelings she had for her husband were gone.

"Thank you, Jesus," Shenae said, looking toward the ceiling.

God can really work miracles when you turn yourself over to Him, she thought.

After her shower, she towel dried her natural tresses. She'd wear a full afro today to celebrate her independence. She was often seen wearing a hat to cover her hair in church, but today she just didn't feel like bundling herself up. She hoped Angelo would still be at church today. She covered herself up as much as possible just in case Kenya was with him. She wouldn't change herself for anyone, but attempting to curb some of her newfound sensuality might be in order—at least while she was inside the church doors.

When she finally dressed, she spun around in the mirror and thoroughly enjoyed the sight glowing in her reflection. Putting on her nude Manolo Blahnik pumps, she headed toward the door. Leon, to her delight, was gone.

"Thank you, Jesus…again."

Shenae went into her kitchen to eat something before she took some medicine for her headache. She saw her divorce papers on the island in the kitchen and remembered that she was still in need of Leon's signature. Now that he was out of jail and the two of them were on speaking terms, she'd be the one to do what her lawyer hadn't been able to. He'd sign those papers; she'd make sure of it.

"And thank you, Jesus, in advance," Shenae said, beaming at the thought of being a free woman.

She grabbed her keys and headed toward her door. As always, she checked her appearance in the mirror for the last time before turning the doorknob.

"Angelo!" she said, swinging the door open to find him standing there. He looked just as good as she remembered him. He was calmer now though and smiling at her.

"What are you doing here?" she said, noticing the flowers in his hand. "Are those for me?"

Shenae scolded herself for asking such stupid questions. He was at her house to see her, and, of course, the flowers were for her. The things his presence did to her brain were unforgivable.

"They are," he said, handing the bouquet to her. "I came to apologize."

He'd been a jerk and he knew it. He'd overreacted at her simply trying to express herself, and that wasn't fair. She was entitled to her own feelings and emotions. And upon waking up this morning, he'd realized that he wanted to share his feelings and emotions as well…with her.

"Shenae, I was hoping that you and I could have something special one day," Angelo began. "I need you to hear me say that I want to be with you. I'm tired of not saying it to you."

They'd become best friends over these past weeks. And who better to step out on faith with than your best friend?

"I want to see what God has for us. Last night, when you said those things about Leon, I—."

"Leon and I are over," Shenae interrupted him. "There is never going to be a Leon and I again. We have beautiful children, but that chapter is closed."

She saw Angelo's smile get wider, exposing those dimples that she loved so much.

"I was hoping that we could start a new one," Shenae finished.

"And just to be clear, your ex is not a part of this new chapter, right?" Angelo asked, still smiling but his tone was more serious.

"I'm absolutely positive that he will no longer be a problem."

With that promise, it was Shenae who leaned in and kissed Angelo. She wanted to also assure him that she was absolutely not just his friend anymore.

Shenae silently sent another thank you up to the heavens.

Ten thousand tongues wouldn't be enough to thank you, Jesus.

Pun intended.

LYNETTE

Pastor Andre sat at the breakfast bar watching his beautiful wife make Sunday morning breakfast before church. Today, they'd be joining their friends again to officially see Bishop Paden and Amauri off to New York.

He was trying to review the notes of the day's farewell sermon, but the smell of his wife's cooking was a huge distraction.

"That smells so good, First Lady," he told her. "This is why I thank God for you every day."

She smiled back at him.

"Oh, really. Is that the only reason?" she asked.

They laughed together and Pastor Andre noticed he'd missed a call on his cell. It was Harriet who had called.

"Harriet just left me a voicemail," Andre announced to his wife, causing her smile to fade suddenly.

"What did she say?" Lynette asked, preparing herself for the worst.

Pastor Andre put his index finger out and turned away from his wife to listen to the message.

Lynette stacked her husband's pancakes on the plate and brought it to him at the bar. Seeing Pastor Andre put his phone down, she tried to read his expression.

"What did it say?" she asked again.

He motioned for her to join him on the other side where he was sitting.

"Lynn, before we talk about it," he began, grabbing her hands. "I need to know that you will not leave me. You have to know that what happened all that time ago was a mistake. I will never betray our love like that again."

"Andre, it's ok," replied Lynette, trying not to sound too defeated. "When will we be going back to see your son...our son?"

God, you are something else, she said to herself. She looked up to see her husband trying not to crack a smile.

"Sweetheart, I am not that little boy's father."

She playfully hit him and he laughed. "Why would you do that?"

she asked, hitting him again. "Why would you play like that?"

Pastor Andre grabbed her hand when she tried to hit him a third time. He pulled her toward him and kissed her.

"I love our family just the way it is," he said to her. "I'm glad this is all over."

He released her and stood up, grabbing his phone.

"I'm going to call her back to tell her, I wish her well," he said, moving to exit the kitchen. "My prayers are with her. That baby still needs a donor."

"I'll be praying for her too," said Lynette. "But I won't lie and say I don't feel relieved."

"So do I, babe," he told her, coming back to kiss her again. "Let's officially move forward into what God has next for us. If you're by my side, I can't lose."

She smiled at her handsome husband and pastor. "You are so sexy when you get all declarative and prophetic," she whispered, pulling the string on his sweatpants.

She bit his ear and began to kiss his neck. She'd have her pancake and eat it too this morning.

NATASHA

"Mom, you've called Donte like 15 times already," Nivea said to her mother from the passenger's seat. "What happened to waiting until you two were in front of each other? You're being a little thirsty."

"Young lady, if I knew what it meant to be thirsty, I'd have some words for you," Natasha responded, putting her phone back in the cup holder. "I just want to talk to him. He's not answering."

Natasha hated to admit it, but she had called Donte more times than she'd like to admit. It was driving her crazy that he was ignoring her calls. Him ignoring her coupled with this Sunday morning traffic was too much for Natasha to deal with.

She grabbed her phone once more and tried Donte. Again, no answer.

"Mom. Chill," Nivea said, laughing. "Give me the phone."

As they pulled into the parking lot, Natasha saw the place was packed. Everyone had come out for the last farewell. She secretly wished she had that coveted "First Lady" spot she used to. Now, she'd have to spend time finding a spot like everyone else and hike a mile to get in. She hoped Antonio would wait for her in the foyer like she'd asked. She was a woman on a mission this morning and she needed at least one man in her life to act right, even if it was the one whose heart she would have to break.

After walking from the second parking lot, Natasha was more determined than ever. Reaching the church's front doors, she spotted Antonio with his back turned to her. They had about 15 minutes before the start of service and he was waiting patiently. She stayed outside, waiting for him to turn and see her. As soon as he did, a smile crept on Antonio's face and he walked out to meet them.

Antonio swept Nivea into a big hug and twirled her around. Natasha watched her daughter squeal in delight. It was so sweet to see their relationship blossoming like it was.

"Go ahead inside to your youth service," she urged Nivea, hoping she understood that she couldn't stick around for what was about to take place. Her daughter nodded, running off to join her friends.

The first thing Antonio noticed was the absence of the ring on Natasha's finger. He sensed bad news coming for him.

"You aren't wearing your ring," he said, gently grabbing her hand.

Natasha took her hand back and rubbed the empty spot on her

finger before continuing.

"I'm sorry, Antonio," she responded. "I just…I can't—."

"Lemme guess. You can't do this, right?" he interrupted her. "You can, T-Shae. It's just cold feet. "

All he needed was time, time to show her that he was for her.

"You know what? Ignore it. Let's go get some word."

He grabbed for her hand again and tried to pull her toward the doors. When she didn't move, he knew that the news would be more severe than he imagined.

"I really can't do this," Natasha finally said.

"Donte?" he asked her, trying to figure out what had triggered this change of heart.

She nodded in response. He sighed at her confirmation.

"I can't even be mad at you, I guess," he told her. "I figured it was a long shot, but I was starting to have more hope than a little bit."

His hand was still holding hers. Natasha didn't really know what else to say to him. The speech she had prepared this morning was nowhere to be found.

"You know what? We have a beautiful daughter. And I hate that I was so stupid back in my youth, but it is what it is. We still have her," Antonio said to her.

Natasha felt compelled to at least hug him. She reached her hands up for his neck and pulled him close. Whatever they had 18-plus years ago had given them one gift, and now both of them were finally on board to give her the best life they could. She let go and kissed him.

"Thank you for not making it hard," she said to him.

"There will probably be some tears later," he joked. "But I'm a man. You wont see it."

Silently, Natasha thanked God that she didn't have to experience what she thought she would. She walked into the sanctuary with Antonio and found the rest of the Deborah's Daughters who were holding a space for her in their pew.

After the long week that all the ladies had seen, Sunday morning was their time to bring all their cares to the altar and begin anew. After the amazing worship, they were mostly left in tears. God's presence could be felt all throughout the building. He had been with each of them in the midst of their brokenness. And each knew that He would continue to be there. They hadn't forgotten how He'd been there when things were going well for them. In all honesty, they led marvelous lives. They were not only clothed well, but they each had healthy families and beautiful homes. God had always provided for them, and despite their shortcomings, He had granted them mercy.

Amauri was the first to leave her seat to join the collective circle of women. Lynette followed, joining arms, and following her came Natasha and Shenae. The ladies held each other up. Together, they prayed for the hearts in their midst that didn't know Jesus. It was Pastor Andre who was overcome with the most emotion. As he approached the pulpit, the ladies expected a message about forgiveness. But the Lord had other plans.

"I am so blessed to stand before the people of God today," he began. "It is with a humble heart that I am standing here, a marred man myself."

He turned toward Paden before continuing.

"I'd like Bishop Paden to join me. As we were preparing for the growth of the ministry over the past few months, the Lord has ministered to our overseer about the unveiling of giftings. I will let Bishop explain further."

Everyone sat on the edge of their seats as Bishop Paden explained that, over the course of the last five months, many of the members had been in a private training. He explained that one of the members had shown tremendous strides and would be elevated as an associate pastor.

"I am so blessed to call this man not only my son in the ministry but also a friend. Please come forward Pastor Elect Donte Smith."

Everyone stood to their feet in shocked applause. But no one was more shocked than Natasha. She watched him come forward to accept the hand from the Pastoral staff.

"We have seen a mighty move of God in Him," said Bishop Paden, shaking Donte's hand. "And we can't wait for him to come back to us in three months after he finishes his classes to formally appoint him."

Natasha guessed that's what Donte was talking about last night on the phone.

"Somebody give God glory in this place!" Paden called the congregation to action.

The men of God laid hands on his back and prayed for God to use him as they saw fit.

"Now I will give the mic back to Pastor Andre."

Bishop Paden walked Donte down the steps and sat next to him. Natasha hoped that her stares at him would cause him to stare back at her. But he wouldn't budge; his eyes remained forward. It only fueled Natasha's fire to get him back after the service.

"Saints, before I begin, I want to thank God for allowing me this opportunity to stand before you this morning," Pastor Andre began his message. "I want to secondly thank my Rib, your First Lady Lynette. I am so blessed to have her call me Pastor first."

He smiled at his wife, sitting on the front row. Lynette mouthed the words "I love you" at him. This was her favorite part of the sermon, when her husband acknowledged her before the men and women they led. It almost made the early mornings, the late night hospital visits, and the life interruptions worth it. The charge of First Lady wasn't merely about the clothes, but it was a true calling on their lives, full of commitments and responsibilities.

"I am a little unsteady right now, because I prepared a word about forgiveness," Pastor Andre began again. "I was just wrestling with the Holy Spirit as I sat in worship, because He is commanding that I change that."

The ladies all looked perplexed. A wash of curiosity and worry invaded Lynette. She was hoping that she wasn't in for another whirlwind confession from her husband. She looked at him, wanting to ferociously shake her head.

"No worries, honey. I have no earth shattering confessions to make," Pastor Andre assured her, causing the church to erupt in laughter. It was so good that, after such a crazy two years, the pair could laugh. Pastor Andre noted in his head that this was indeed a serious matter and he would never betray his wife's trust again.

"I'm compelled to talk to you about timing this morning," Pastor Andre continued. So many of us have been standing on the outside of life…as if it's a jump rope and we're waiting for our turn to jump. Many of us have jumped too soon and have tripped and fallen. The ropes of life are turning, and instead of jumping in, we've allowed the apprehension of what will come next to hold us back. Some of us have jumped in knowing that it wasn't time and then we've had to jump out because we failed. God is saying that in His time, things will move as they should..."

The scripture for the sermon was Ecclesiastics 3: 11: He hath made every thing beautiful in his time: also he hath set the world in their heart, so that no man can find out the work that God maketh from the beginning to the end.

Pastor Andre went on to minister about how, instead of trying to anticipate God's next move, we should celebrate that, in God's time, it will be made perfect. Each of the Daughters applied that word to their lives and thought about where they each stood. Natasha felt more confirmed than ever that her time with Donte had come.

"Now as I bring this message to a close, I want to minister to those that don't have a personal relationship with God..."

Natasha heard Pastor Andre about to end the service and looked to where Donte had been sitting. He was no longer at the end of her pew. When Pastor Andre called the families of the church forward for prayer, Nivea joined her mother and Antonio at the altar. The three held hands as both of Nivea's parents promised to fulfill the oath of parenthood that God had bestowed upon them.

"Have you seen Donte?" Natasha asked Lynette, frantically scanning the sanctuary after the service.

"No, I haven't actually," responded Lynette. "But Andre is sure to know. I'm on my way to meet him in the visitor's suite to greet the first time guests. We'll be out in about 15 to 20 minutes."

"Twenty minutes?!" Natasha exclaimed. "He could be halfway around the world by then, Lynn."

Lynette looked at her friend, concerned. She would hate to see her lose Donte again after all she'd been through lately.

"Well check the parking lot to see if his car is still there. If it is, then he's bound to be somewhere in the church," Lynette said, pleased with her brilliance.

She hugged Natasha and turned her toward the front doors.

"There's hope," Natasha heard Lynette say to her. "There's always hope. Now go."

Natasha rushed out among the sea of people, pushing past them to the parking lot. She ran over to where Donte usually parked when he drove them to church. His truck wasn't there.

"No," Natasha whispered. "No, no, no."

She spun around to head back inside, reaching for her cell phone in her purse. She'd call him and he'd answer this time. He just had to. Looking down, she nearly ran over a woman in a long, velvet frock.

"Oh my goodness, I'm so sorry," Natasha said, looking up to find she'd bumped into Kenya, Angelo's sister.

"No, it's ok," Kenya said, clearly annoyed.

What was up with this lady and these long dresses?, Natasha thought to herself. She looked past Kenya to see Amauri and Bishop Paden exiting the church, surrounded by people trying to say their final goodbyes.

They rounded the corner, getting closer now to where Kenya and Natasha were standing. Kenya got sight of Paden and felt the familiar ache of jealousy hit her in the stomach. She was sick taking in the picture perfect life he had: his blonde bombshell, his two daughters, and his three churches. All she had was a closet full of body-covering smocks and a brother for a roommate.

Kenya had come to church to warn him that, in her anger, she'd found a way to reach his brother in New York the night before. She felt horrible that she might have put him in danger and wanted to warn him. But she knew that white woman probably wouldn't let her anywhere near him now. She wasn't sure how long she watched Bishop Paden, kissing the children and hugging the members goodbye before she'd taken all she could.

"How well do you know Bishop Paden?" Natasha asked Kenya, startling her.

She'd seen that look of love before on a woman. Something was up.

"Uh, we grew up together," responded Kenya, scolding herself for being so obvious.

"Hmmm," Natasha noted.

Kenya thought to hurriedly change the subject.

"Your name's Natasha, right? Aren't you looking for someone?"

"Yeah. I've been looking for Donte all over the place. Have you seen him?"

Kenya nodded her head.

"If you're talking about the bald guy in white from last night, he just pulled out in his truck and left right before you bumped into me," recalled Kenya.

"Ugh, I knew it," said an alarmed Natasha.

She could see Amauri and Paden about to enter their vehicle. She decided to call out to Paden like a madwoman.

"Bishop, I need your help!" she yelled.

Paden looked in the direction of the voice he heard and saw Natasha standing next to a woman who looked like Kenya. Upon seeing him look over in her direction, Kenya bolted in the other direction toward the adjacent lot where she'd parked.

"Bishop!" Natasha yelled again, running over to him. "I need to get to Donte. Where is he?"

She poured her heart out to him, admitting that she'd been crazy to think that God wouldn't send the man of her dreams in the most unlikely package.

"I pushed him away, but I need him to know that I love him," she said, catching everyone's attention by this point. "I love him and I want to be his wife. I don't care about the money. I just want him."

Lynette and Shenae had joined the crowd outside now. Amauri squeezed Paden's hand, alerting him to do the right thing for her friend.

"Natasha, marriage is serious," Paden told her. "And considering all you've been through in these last two years, I need you to know you are ready. Two unhealed people can harm each other, even if their intentions are right."

He looked at Natasha, searching her face. Paden meant business. He'd counseled premarital couples, post-marital couples, and married couples in the heat of the storm. He certainly didn't take the vows that he explained to them lightly.

"What does God say, Natasha?" he asked.

"God says, 'He that findeth a wife findeth a good thing.' I'm telling you, Bishop, I am that man's good thing. I am his favor."

"I want you to say it again, Natasha," Bishop Paden urged. "Tell me why you think that Donte is the one for you. There are many witnesses around. And most importantly, God is listening."

"When I met Donte years ago, I knew he was a good man," Natasha felt the words flowing out of her like milk. "I honestly thought that he was too good for me. When Pastor Shawn came asking to court me, I thought that he was what God wanted for me."

She went on to explain that she and Shawn had struggled for so long until Natasha couldn't stand it anymore. So she became who her husband wanted her to be.

"And for the record, I didn't want my husband to die. I loved him and I loved that he took the time out to give my baby the world," she said, hoping that she had the attention of members from her old congregation. "When he died, I'd never felt so lost. I didn't know who to be anymore. But Donte has never asked me to be anyone but myself. He prays for me, he was a friend when I needed one the most, and he never gave up on me."

She stopped after that sentence, feeling tears about to overwhelm her.

"...Well, he never gave up until now," she said. "But I want him to know I haven't given up on us. I realized that being with him, I didn't have to be anyone but who God made me. I'm ready, Bishop, to be his wife. I promise, Bishop, I'm ready."

Everyone in the crowd was moved. Many had heard the stories of Pastor Shawn and Natasha. It was sad that instead of embracing that life moves on, many of his members were stuck in the mentality that mourning should be for a lifetime.

"Mom!" Natasha heard the voice of her daughter somewhere in the crowd.

"Niv?"

She saw the crowd part a bit to reveal her daughter, smiling from ear to ear. Holding her hand was Donte. He'd been there the whole time.

Natasha felt her heart jump from her chest in joy.

"Did you mean it?" Donte asked, looking into the eyes of the woman that he loved more than life itself.

"Yes," she said, tears running down her face. For the first time in forever it seemed, she was crying because she was happy.

"I meant every word. Donte, I love you so much," she told him, running into his arms.

"Natasha, I've waited so long to hear you say that to me," he said, his face buried in her hair.

Shenae's eyes filled with tears. Her sister was finally going to get her happy ending. She put her arms around Angelo's waist and pulled him close. She was hopeful that hers was in the making as well.

Amauri clung to the arm of her husband, glad that they could be apart of something so beautiful before they left for their new adventure. Lynette was glad that amongst all the dysfunction in their lives, beauty had finally reared its head. She didn't have a magic ball to tell her what would become of her life after all she'd experienced, but as long as she had her incredible husband, she felt like she could do anything. She nuzzled into Andre's neck and squeezed his butt cheek for effect.

Nivea was crying almost as hard as her mother was. She'd witnessed her survive the hardest struggles, and now she was finally realizing what Natasha meant when she said, "I'm happy if you're happy." The joy she felt from her mother's decision was overwhelming.

Donte bent to his knee for the second time in front of Natasha.

"I want to spend the rest of my life showing you how much I love you. Will you do the honor of being my wife?"

Without hesitation, Natasha screamed, "Yes!"

EPILOGUE: 3 months later

NATASHA

The wedding and reception had gone by too fast, recalled Natasha, reclining on the patio of their honeymoon suite in Punta Cana.

When Bishop Paden had said the words, "You may now kiss your bride," something seemed to click in Donte. He'd captured Natasha's lips and the room went silent as he took the liberties he now had to enjoy his rib. The catcalls and whistles let Natasha know that the attendees too saw the immediate switch in their usually reserved Pastor Donte. But she wasn't complaining.

He'd been ordained the week before the wedding, and everything else was a whirlwind. Bishop Paden had asked if the couple could accompany them to New York as the assistant pastors of Covenant Christian Ministries. It was a resounding yes as they were both ready to start their new life together.

But for now, as she looked out onto the shores of the Dominican Republic, it was just the two of them in this beautiful private suite. The entire flight, Donte had teased her, kissed her, and promised a night to remember.

He had planned everything honeymoon related, so Natasha had just agreed to be spontaneous for once in her life. He'd even taken the liberty of leaving all the clothes that she'd picked out for their honeymoon at home. He'd packed his own suitcase for her, which left her a little uneasy, but she trusted him. Knowing that he'd approved all the bags' contents by Shenae and Lynette, Natasha begged her bridesmaids to tell her what he'd included in the pink luggage set he'd bought for her.

She checked her watch, remembering that he'd told her to give him 10 minutes to set everything up in the bedroom for their first intimate night together. That was five minutes ago, and Natasha could wait no longer.

She rose to find her new hubby inside. He was sprinkling red and white rose petals all over their bedroom.

"Hey," Donte said, throwing the last of the petals upon seeing his bride. "You're early."

"Why red and white?" she asked him, stepping into the bedroom.

"They mean unity. Tonight we become one."

Maybe it was the way he said it or the kiss he planted on her lips after he said it. Either way, Natasha knew she was about to be romanced like she'd never been before. He swept her in his arms and kissed her, running his fingers up and down the sides of her dress. He grabbed her bottom. A low growl escaped her mouth in appreciation.

"Are you sure you're up for this?" Natasha asked, playfully backing away from his hands.

"Oh, I've been ready a long time," Donte said, grabbing her hand and running it down the course of his slacks so she could see what she did to him.

He'd admitted to her in premarital counseling that he'd been celibate for 10 years. Natasha wasn't sure how he'd done it. Her little two years paled in comparison.

"Wow," she said, giggling. "You are ready."

She took his lips again and backed him toward the bed. Looking at him as she slipped off his tank, she could tell that he was more than prepared to handle what would come next.

"Wait, babe," he said, stopping her.

He pointed toward the corner of the room where the doorman had dropped their bags.

"Put on Saturday," he ordered.

Saturday?, Natasha thought. Wow. He'd put a lot of thought into this. She opened the bag to see that he'd wrapped each outfit in tissue paper marked with a day of the week. She noticed, though, that a day was missing.

After dressing, she came out of the master bathroom and heard Donte gasp when he saw her. He was taking her in, white bustier, matching panties, and all. He'd chosen a perfect fit for her. She felt like a Hollywood pin up model, and she was glad to offer that fantasy to her husband.

"God, you look amazing," he said in admiration, his voice almost a whisper once they were close enough to touch. "I am going to enjoy getting this off of you"

She laughed.

"Sweetheart, I'm missing a day."

"What day, love?" he asked.

"Sunday."

"Oh, that's because I've reserved that day for costumes."

"Excuse me?"

"I've decided we will be Adam and Eve that day, pre-forbidden fruit."

The couple laughed so hard, it broke any first-time tension they had. Seeing her laugh for joy turned him on again, and the kiss that followed was nothing like the chaste kisses that he'd showered her with all day.

The two wrestled intensely with each other. He'd try to own her with his kisses while she'd fight back to show him that she was eager as well. When she felt his hands cupping her breasts, she thought she'd nearly explode. Donte pulled at her exposed nipples hard enough to awaken them. She felt heat and wetness inside her, his hand roaming inside her silk panties. He was taking his time. He insisted on taunting her with the pressure against her peak. She'd foolishly thought that his lack of practice would have given her the upper hand. She was wrong. He moved to trail kisses down her neck to collar bone. Natasha nearly wept from the passion of it. He picked her up and laid her across the bed. She gripped the sheets on either side of her, ready to see what he was working with.

Instead of undressing, Donte grabbed a blindfold and the bucket of strawberries off the nightstand.

He handed her the blindfold, his eyes filled with mischief. "You want to blindfold me...on our first time?" Natasha asked.

She felt herself get moist at the thought of what he'd do to her once she put it on. He nodded in response to her question, his hands continuing to roam her body. As she moved to tie the black piece of fabric over her eyes, Donte massaged her thighs. His hands were warm against her skin and the oil he used only sent more shivers up her body. She arched against him, now completely in the dark, her other senses were very much elevated.

"Open your mouth," his baritone voice commanded. She wondered if he was going to let her taste him first. Her mouth watered at the thought of him placing the length of him inside her mouth.

Natasha obliged, opening her mouth to taste the sweetness of the strawberry, and then his lips were there again. Now she could feel the coolness of the fruit against her breast before the warmth of his mouth possessed her. He was cherishing the sweetness of her mixed with the taste of the berry's juice. She could feel herself becoming full aroused. He must have sensed it too because he stopped.

She felt him shifting on the bed and figured he was finally removing his clothes to let the real fun begin. In a flash, his mouth was on her second set of lips. She moaned louder than she meant to.

"You taste so good," Donte said, taking the time to savor the flavors his wife gave him. Her moans taunted him to pick up the pace, but he would not. He'd waited too long to have her, and he'd erase every memory of any other man who ever touched her. He kissed her, and this time, his fingers played inside of her. Natasha nearly gasped as he explored her. He was commanding her body to respond now. She could feel the building tension; her fingers were digging deep into his back, begging him not to stop. Donte wanted to see her face as he made her climax. He snatched the blindfold off and watched her writhe in passion. It was beautiful; her body shivered and he swore she looked like she was about to levitate off the bed.

"Remember, this is what only I can do to you," he said, gently tapping away at her spot, watching her cum for him.

He smiled an erotic smile of ecstasy when she fell back in elation.

"Now, let me show you what I can really do," he said.

AMAURI

Amauri was so glad that she and Paden had flown back to Atlanta to perform the wedding ceremony for Donte and Natasha. She was even more excited that her sister would be moving to New York with them. Their family would make a perfect addition to the ministry.

She passed by Paden's new home office on her way to check on their daughters. She peeked in to see him tapping away at the keyboard, as usual.

"I love you, B.P.," she whispered, causing him to stop what he was doing and look at her.

"I love you more, First Lady," he said.

He blew her a kiss and she caught it.

"Hey, let's order in tonight and watch a movie with the girls," he offered. "We haven't done that in a while."

"Sounds good, babe. Just let me know when you're done working and I'll call it in."

Satisfied, Amauri ran off to leave her husband in peace. As soon as he could no longer hear her footsteps, Paden's phone rang.

"Hello?" Bishop Paden answered.

"Pade. It's me, Money," said the voice of Paden's brother on the line.

Paden almost choked in response. His brother was supposed to be in jail. What was he doing calling him? And how did he even get his number?

"I heard you ran into Kenya a few months ago," Money continued. "She told me that you stayed with that pretty snowflake. Guess you'll never learn, Pade. Guess I'll have to re-teach you that lesson, boy."

"Money, I will not allow you to harm my family," Bishop Paden said, starting to become angry; he didn't respond well to threats.

"We settled this years ago," Bishop Paden told his brother. "I left the life. I got out."

"This whole God stuff is a front, Pade. Or at least it was supposed to be. But now, you've gone and married the snow bunny, had half-snowflake kids by her, and lost touch with the homies."

"Money—."

"The homies aren't pleased, Pade. Please believe there will be Hell to pay."

Bishop Paden hung up, slamming the receiver so loud that the entire phone crashed to the ground. The sound caused Amauri to run back into her husband's office.

"Paden?" she asked, rushing to her husband's side. "What's wrong? Who was that?"

"Amauri...," began Bishop Paden.

He was shaking as he spoke.

"Amauri, I have to tell you something." The next sound the two heard was the crash of broken glass upstairs. They dropped to the floor as they heard gunshots ring through their front windows.

THE END

I am so glad that you took this journey with me! These characters are my sisters and brothers in Christ. I am as invested in their wellbeing as you are.

Rocks, Rings, and Resurrections! Wow!

Stay tuned for Secrets, Sinners, and Saints!

We'll finally find out who Bishop Paden really is and why he never told Amauri about her assailant.

And Natasha and Donte, everyone's favorite pair, are now newly-weds. Will they ride off into the sunset? Maybe not!

First Ladies Club: Rocks, Rings and Resurrections

Made in the USA
Charleston, SC
28 November 2014